OUT
OF THE
BLACKOUT
ROBERT
BARNARD

A DELL BOOK

Published by
Dell Publishing
a division of
Bantam Doubleday Dell Publishing Group, Inc.
666 Fifth Avenue
New York, New York 10103

First published in the United States by Charles Scribner's Sons 1985.

ISBN: 0-440-16761-2
Reprinted by arrangement with Charles Scribner's Sons

Printed in the United States of America
Published simultaneously in Canada

One Previous Dell Edition
October 1989

10 9 8 7 6 5 4 3 2 1

KRI

OUT
OF THE
BLACKOUT

CHAPTER 1

When the train containing the children pulled into Yeasdon Station it was nearly four hours late. Several among the little knot of people waiting to meet them had become restive: one man said—almost hopefully, it seemed—that it didn't look as if they were *going* to come at all; and one woman said that her George would be wanting his tea. These eruptions of shuffling and discontent were given short shrift by Mrs Sellerman.

'Your George can get his own tea for once,' she said. 'After all, there *is* a war on.'

Mrs Sellerman saw it as her duty to keep up the spirits of the waiting foster families, and she kept up a constant stream of bright commentary and admonition: it would be so bewildering for the poor little things she said, shunted off to a strange place, away from their homes and their mothers, many of them in the country for the first time in their lives, very probably. It was up to them, she proclaimed, to make them feel *safe* and *welcome*. It was the least they could do.

Takes too much on herself, does Nan Sellerman, was the unspoken thought in many a waiting breast. For though she was a kindly woman, and a capable one, this first taste of responsibility had rather gone to Mrs Sellerman's head, and had certainly made her more than a little sententious. But the thought remained unspoken, for this was 1941, and her place in the upper ranks of the village hierarchy protected Mrs Sellerman from outright criticism.

So everyone was still there when the train drew in. The children leapt and ran and rolled off it, shouting and laughing and displaying very few signs of disorientation. Mrs Sellerman, aided by Mr Thurston the headmaster and Mr Wise the vicar, quickly got them together into a little group—twenty or more, there were—outside the waiting-room, and prepared to allot them to their new homes and their temporary guardians. Mr Thurston insisted on making a little speech of welcome (he was all too fond of little speeches, which usually, like Topsy, growed), and while he was talking about 'these difficult times' and 'all doing their bit,' Mrs Sellerman surveyed the children. A few were quite respectably dressed and still fairly neat, but most of them were in the range from the untidy to the frankly deplorable.

'I know they've had a long journey,' said Mrs Sellerman under her breath to the vicar, 'but you'd think some of the mothers could have made a bit more effort. In times like these . . . '

Mr Wise saw no oddity in regarding tidy children as part of the war effort. He murmured: 'Remember, they will not be at all the sort of children we are used to here. Slum children, you know . . . '

For Mr Wise, and for most of the people of Yeasdon, all children from big cities who did not come from impeccably middle-class backgrounds were 'slum children.'

At that point a boy in the group, a heavy-limbed lout of fully nine years, rather proved his point by shouting:

'Stow it, mister. We're 'ungry.'

Mr Thurston brought his remarks speedily to an end, and took from Nan Sellerman the list of names.

'Ah yes, now. Who's first? Sally Bates—you're to go with Mr and Mrs Carter. Mary Nicholls—you'll be living with Miss Petheridge. Are you there, Miss Petheridge? Good—this little girl is Mary. Yes, do take her along now. Terence Stope—oh no, Terence isn't coming, after all. William Smithson . . . '

And so it went on. One by one the children, sobered a little as they were separated from the rest, trotted off with their foster parents, to be caught up in linguistic entanglements as cockney met West Country, to be bewildered by the smells and spaciousness of the countryside, cheered by the unaccustomed lavishness of country fare, and in some cases to be terrified by the first bath of their young lives.

Mostly they were tough kids, and cheerful, and while they commented rather disdainfully on everything that was different from home, they seemed ready enough to adapt.

'Ere, they say there's not even a *cinema* here,' said one, as he was taken off by a local farmer.

'Still, at least there won't be any air raids,' said another.

'Worse luck!' shouted the heavy-limbed boy, still uncollected from the group. 'Zoo-oo-oom! Kerr-rash!'

In the space of twenty minutes Mr Thurston came to the last name on his list, and Ellen Tucker was taken off by a nervous retired couple who had put away all their ornaments in a high cupboard preparatory to her arrival. Rural peace began to descend on Yeasdon Station.

'Well, that seems to be that,' said Mr Thurston, removing his spectacles. 'And I think we can congratulate ourselves—'

'Er—Mr Thurston—' said Mrs Sellerman. He looked in her direction, and she gestured towards a small boy, still standing near the door of the waiting-room, a diminutive case clasped in his hand.

'Oh dear!' said Mr Thurston, fussily donning his spectacles again. 'Have I missed one? One, two, three . . . No, I've been through them all. Ah—I have it: you must be Terence Stope. I heard your mummy wouldn't part with you, but she's decided to send you after all, has she? Very sensible of her.'

The boy looked up at him thoughtfully.

'No,' he said.

'Not Terence? Or Terry? Do they call you Terry?'

'No,' said the little boy. 'I'm Simon. Simon . . . Thorn.'

He was a pensive, reserved child, perhaps five or six years old. He was neater than the average child in the group: his clothes were far from new, but that was not unusual in that year of grace 1941, and Simon's were clean and pressed and newly darned. He wore grey short trousers, grey socks, and a fawn pullover with a little blue band knitted into the V-neck. Home-knitted, Nan Sellerman's appraising eye told her, not bought. He was less skinny than many of the others, and certainly suffered from none of the diseases of malnutrition or poor heredity that one or two of them had been burdened with.

'Simon Thorn . . . Simon Thorn,' said Mr Thurston with concern, and he consulted his list yet again. 'No, you're definitely not on the list. Goodness me—how can that have happened? Did they send you when Terence Stope dropped out, I wonder? *Most* inconsiderate not to have informed me—but then, these last few nights in London have been so dreadful . . . Well, what's to be done? Tomorrow I shall have to telephone to Hackney. But in the meanwhile . . . ?'

'If I may make a suggestion, Mr Thurston,' put in Mrs Sellerman, tentatively. Mr Thurston was a perfectly good-natured man, but the village was somewhat in awe of him, as they were of all teachers. 'Mr and Mrs Cutheridge were awfully disappointed when they heard that Terence Stope wasn't coming. He'd been assigned to them, you know. They're childless—a really nice, responsible couple . . . '

She turned to the vicar in search of confirmation.

'They're Methodists,' Mr Wise murmured, 'but as far as I know, yes . . . '

'Ah!' said Mr Thurston. 'Well, that would seem to be the the solution. Until we can sort things out, find out the position . . . ' He turned to the little boy. 'You are *sure* you're not Terence Stope, aren't you?'

'I'm Simon Thorn,' said the boy, now with more confidence.

'Yes, well, we'll see to it that you're all right. I suppose this Mr Cutheridge is not on the telephone?'

'Oh, I wouldn't think so, Mr Thurston. He's stockman to Sir Henry.'

'Ah—no, of course. Now I wonder who could take him along.'

'I'll go with him,' said Mrs Sellerman. 'It's not above a mile.'

And so the little difficulty was sorted out, for that night at least. Simon Thorn and Mrs Sellerman trudged through the darkening village, the little boy walking determinedly, and looking around eagerly as if to impress this first, dim view of Yeasdon on his memory. 'Is this all the houses there are?' he asked at one point. Before long they came to a substantial cottage just beyond the outskirts of the village, a cottage tied to Sir Henry Beesley's estate. Mrs Cutheridge was surprised to open the door to Nan Sellerman and a little boy, after her disappointment of the day before, but the matter was soon explained. Dot Cutheridge displayed openly a quiet satisfaction which concealed a deep inner delight. Simon was hustled into the warm, close atmosphere of the cottage, was sat up at the table by Tom Cutheridge (who was big and homely and smelt of barns), and was given a great plate of Lancashire hot-pot (Mrs Cutheridge, that evening, had only ham and bread and butter). Then he was given a bath by the fire in a little tin tub, and was soon put lovingly to bed. He was clearly exhausted. He fell asleep almost at once. Dot Cutheridge knew, because she listened at the door.

Mr Thurston and the evacuees' committee had plenty on their plates next morning, so that Simon, so quiet and well settled, was the least of their problems. One boy had already run away (it was one of the ones who had been given their first bath), but some of the others had made themselves all too thoroughly at home. So it was not until midday that Mr Thurston found time to telephone through to Hackney. It was then that he became aware—for in the sudden uprush of activity caused by the evacuees' arrival he had missed both the nine o'clock news and the early morning news that day—that during the evening and night of May 10th London had been bombed as savagely as at any time during the war to date.

Eventually he got through to the school the children had attended. They had sent no extra boy to replace Terence Stope. Then he rang through to the Town Hall. They were running an emergency service only, due to bombing the night before, and his call was interrupted by another air-raid siren. When finally, in the late afternoon, he spoke to the overworked official responsible for the party, he was unable to explain the surplus boy. There had originally been twenty-two children on the list. The refusal of Terence Stope's mother to part with him left twenty-one. His place had not been filled by any other child. Of the twenty-one, eighteen had come from the Bradlaugh Street Primary School, three from the Jubilee Green Primary School. The children had been put into their carriages on the special train by a teacher from Bradlaugh Street. Naturally there would have been a few children she had never seen before.

'Will you check your records, then, to see if you have anywhere a boy called Simon Thorn?' asked Mr Thurston, mystified, but not at this stage worried.

'Records!' said the official. 'We'll do what we can, of course. It's chaos here, as you can imagine—offices being bombed, things being shifted God knows where. There's plenty of records have gone up in flames, though none of the education ones, so far as I know.'

But when the man at Hackney Town Hall rang back the next day, he had found no trace at all of a Simon Thorn.

Meanwhile Simon himself had settled in nicely. Mrs Cutheridge pronounced him 'a love of a child', and glowed in his company. She had discovered that he had no ration book with him, and had already commenced battle with officialdom to get him one. Tom Cutheridge said he was 'that sharp', and had already shown him round Sir Henry's estate, and given him a ride on one of the old shire horses. At school Simon was pronounced 'a good little reader' and 'quite forward for his age'—which no one quite knew, but which he said was five.

None of which solved the problem of who Simon was, or how he had come to be there in Yeasdon. After some frustrating days of telephoning in the intervals he had from teaching (for twenty-one extra pupils caused great disruption in a village school, particularly sharp, mischievous, cunning town children), Mr Thurston took to writing letters.

But if telephoning into a London blitzed into near-chaos was difficult, writing was hardly more satisfactory. Sometimes he got a reply, sometimes he did not. He established that there had been one other train for evacuees leaving Paddington at around the same time as the one for Yeasdon, but when, after innumerable frustrations and misconnections, he talked with the teacher who had gone with that train, now evacuated to rural Oxfordshire, she told him there had been no child missing from her group, and nobody by the name of Simon Thorn was known to her. When, eventually, he wrote again to Hackney to ask them to check up on the boy called Terence Stope, he had a letter back to say that Terence, with his mother, had been killed in a raid two weeks after Simon Thorn had arrived in Yeasdon.

People began to talk. Some of the foster parents asked their billeted kids if they knew who Simon Thorn was. Oh yes, they all knew who he was: he went to school with them in Yeasdon. Yes, but had they known him *before* they were evacuated? None of them had ever seen him before that momentous journey from Paddington Station. Then one of the foster mothers had a bright idea. The Hackney boy who was now mixing fairly happily with, and lording it over, her own children had been one of the last to be collected from the group. His name was Simon. And on the station platform, just beside the waiting-room outside which they had all been assembled, was a thorn bush. What if . . . ?

The mother kept this idea to herself for several days, but when no solution was in sight to the mystery of who was Simon Thorn, she mentioned it to Mrs Sellerman.

Obviously they had to talk to Simon himself.

But here they came up against the barrier of Dot Cutheridge, who was a formidable countrywoman, and very protective.

'It'll all sort itself out,' she said, comfortably. 'He's got a good mother, that anyone can see from the state of his clothes. She'll make sure she finds out where he is. It's some official up there who's got himself into a right ol' tangle. What do you want to go worriting the poor child for?'

But when she said this, Mrs Cutheridge was not revealing all she thought on the subject. For she had wondered—over and over, if the truth be known—whether Simon's mother might not have been killed in an air raid after Simon had left for the station, or on any one of those terrible nights of early May. And wondering did lead to hoping, sinful though she knew this to be. Still, in the long run, even Dot Cutheridge had to back down, and concede that some sort of unofficial investigation would have to take place.

'But I'm not having you bully the child,' she said, and she sat in on all the questioning.

Simon's possessions, Mrs Sellerman found, were unexceptionable but sparse. A change of outer clothing and a spare vest and underpants. A pair of pyjamas. No spare socks or tie. A flannel, but no soap, or toothpaste, or towel. A Teddy-bear, and a large model of the Royal Scot locomotive. Several model cars. There was a little drawing pad, but no name on it, or school. It had pictures of houses, large flowers with an immense sun behind them, and some matchstick people. On one page there was the beginning of a story: 'There was once a boy cald James who went to the moon.' The story petered out after two or three sentences. Mrs Sellerman said to the Rev. Wise, who was helping her with the investigation, that there were very few clothes to an awful lot of children's things, almost as though he'd packed himself. Because the toys must have taken up most of the space in the tiny suitcase.

'It doesn't quite fit with the care she's taken of his clothes,' she said. 'And then not to send his ration book!'

'But then, Londoners,' said Mr Wise.

When Simon was asked, he said he lived in Sparrow Street. He didn't know where Sparrow Street was, but that was where he lived. Or if not *in* Sparrow Street, just off Sparrow Street. He lived with his Mummy. What was his Mummy called? Why, Mummy of course. And there were others in the house—Grandma, and Auntie and, oh, others. Nothing in the way of names could be got out of him at all. They asked him what Sparrow Street was like, and he said it had houses down both sides. Was there anything notable nearby? Anywhere he liked to go? Oh yes, there was a sweetshop, but he didn't remember what street that was in. Did he go to school? Yes, he went to school. Where was the school? Just down the road. What was the name of the school? Simon said that at home they just called it school.

The investigation committee went off to make what they could of this information. Dot Cutheridge imagined them scanning street maps of London for Sparrow Street, and that indeed was what they did. They found only one, and the Rev. Wise, on one of his rare wartime visits to his club in London, actually made his way there. It was in the Alexandra Palace area, and it contained a gas works and three houses, one of them bombed and empty. Neither of the other two housed anyone by the name of Thorn, nor did anyone in the two streets leading off from it know anyone of that name. Sparrow Street was a washout.

Mrs Cutheridge had rather thought it would be. She was getting a very good idea of how Simon's mind worked, and even during the questioning she had remembered how earlier that morning her Tom had been telling Simon the names of the birds in the back garden.

Mrs Cutheridge, in fact, was beginning in her level-headed, commonsensical way to be confident. Simon was a lovely child, she knew that, and loving too. Nothing could be warmer or nicer than his gratitude for all she did for him, for the wonderful farmhouse food she cooked, for the clothes she managed to buy, or procure the material to make. Soon—and this was even better—gratitude was replaced by a simple acceptance: he took it as a matter of course that she and Tom were his protectors and providers. And though Tom said often enough: 'We mustn't build up our hopes,' everybody knew he had built them up long ago. As he often used to say at work: 'We've become a family.'

Not that everything was sunlight. There had been one drawback to Dot's happiness in those first few weeks, one troubling incident, one fright. This, of course, she had told no one, and neither had Tom. The first nights after he had arrived, Simon had slept well—almost too well. The sleep of exhaustion, Dot had called it; she had been a nursery maid up at Sir Henry's, and she knew exhausted children when she saw them. 'All them raids, night after night,' she said, 'tiring him out. Poor little soul.'

But as Simon settled down, she made sure he paced himself better: active enough, but not too active. Then his nights were sometimes more restless. Downstairs, listening to a wireless turned very low, Dot heard him cry out—a whimper, like a dreaming puppy's. She soon realized that his sleep was filled with dreams, not all of them pleasant. In some of them, to judge by his movements and his exclamations, he seemed positively afraid. And then in one of them he cried out—as he was to cry out perhaps once every two or three months for the first year or more after his coming to Yeasdon. The first time she heard it, Dot Cutheridge was standing at the stairhead, listening by the open door, and Tom was shifting uneasily from foot to foot at the bottom of the stairs. The boy had cried out earlier, and now the words that came from him were far from clear—were stifled, it seemed, by terror. But Dot over the early weeks had got used to Simon's speech—some childish habits, some Londonisms. She swore she understood him now, as he cried out in his sleep, and Tom believed her:

'Don't!' the boy called Simon had shouted. 'Don't do that! Stop it—please stop it! Don't hit her! Don't kill her! DON'T!'

CHAPTER 2

Simon Thorn never set foot in London again until the Autumn of nineteen-fifty-six.

By then he was known to everyone as Simon Cutheridge. For a time his friends at school and people in the village had called him Thorn or Cutheridge indiscriminately; gradually, as he became so evidently a part of the family, they all settled down to the latter. But the Cutheridges did not, in those early years, make any attempt to adopt him legally, thinking that to do so would be to tempt fortune, to invite inquiries, perhaps to incur publicity that would bring down Nemesis upon them. In spite of their fears, there was never a challenge, in all the years of Simon's boyhood. When he was eighteen, a small notice was put in the local paper making his assumption of their name legal.

For a reason less logical, more superstitious, Dot and Tom Cutheridge would never take him to London. For most of the inhabitants of Yeasdon and the surrounding villages a trip to London was an occasional treat. What danger the Cutheridges could have anticipated from the programme of these coach trips—the Ideal Home Exhibition, a visit to St Paul's Cathedral, seats for *The Winslow Boy* or the revival of *An Inspector Calls*—can hardly be imagined by anyone for whom the Metropolis does not, of itself, spell danger. And Tom Cutheridge was now head stockman to Sir Henry, who was a good boss. But the Cutheridges never did go on any of these excursions, nor did Simon ever ask to go. Instead, in their little pre-war Austin Seven, they went to Bristol, to Bath or to Exeter.

Simon had been accounted bright from the beginning, and before long he was accredited with something more tangible than brightness. 'The boy's got a brain,' said Mr Thurston, who, for all his prosiness, was an excellent headmaster. He added: 'And he's got the character to use it sensibly.' Mr Thurston never had any doubt that Simon would pass the eleven-plus, and he did it effortlessly. Eight years later it was one of the proudest moments of the headmaster's retirement, only a few months before he died, when he heard that one of 'his' children had won a scholarship to Oxford.

A slight lung defect made the medics declare Simon Grade 3 for National Service, and he was never called up. He went up to Wadham in the autumn of 1956 to study Zoology.

Those who went up to university in 1956 were predestined to be political. In later life Simon Cutheridge quite often did not bother to vote at all, or voted Liberal, but at Oxford he was catapulted into commitment. Not many weeks after he had gone up, while he was still settling in, getting used to having a scout, wondering whether to lose his West Country accent or not, the British, French and Israeli governments invaded Suez. For months Jimmy Porter had been bellowing from the stage of the Royal Court that there were no brave causes to die for any more. Here, suddenly was one. Within days the Russians had moved their tanks into Budapest, and the passionate fury of the undergraduates boiled over. Simon shouted, waved banners, fought in the streets. He stood on platforms haranguing crowds of townspeople and undergraduates through megaphones; he had water poured over him from the windows of St John's. He sat in a little room in the Union watching Hugh Gaitskell's broadcast, and he came close to crying. 'What can we do?' he said to himself, over and over again.

'What can we do?' he asked of a friend, as they left the Union building and he flung a scarf around his throat to keep out the dank November night air.

'We're going to Westminster to lobby our MPs,' said his friend. 'A whole gang of us. Why don't you come?'

'Count me in,' said Simon.

Cocooned in that gang—banner-brandishing, bescarfed fellow students—Simon was carried through Paddington

Station almost without his noticing it. They all charged down into the Underground, and within the hour they were with hundreds more, demonstrating outside the Houses of Parliament. Stolid policemen, part of a good, dying tradition, placed themselves immovably between surge and countersurge of protest and support. Simon and several of the others got into the Palace to lobby their MPs. The member for Simon's constituency was an inarticulate Tory backwoods baronet, who could nevertheless summon up some sort of vocabulary when his passions were roused. He told Simon to his face that he was a conchie, a traitor, and the scum of the earth. Simon was delighted—exhilarated with his success. He repeated the words over and over, to anyone who would listen, and felt cheated when he came across someone whose MP had told him he should be horsewhipped.

The action shifted, as the action always does on these occasions. Before long they were up in Trafalgar Square, and in the thick of demonstrations and counter-demonstrations. A Labour shadow spokesman was speaking from the rostrum, and Simon roared in his support—though the mild-mannered politician seemed more bewildered than gratified by the passion and the fury he aroused. Simon was on the edge of the crowd, and here scuffles and open brawls developed. Mosley's men were enjoying a resurgence, and there were members of the League of Empire Loyalists with loud-hailers. Simon got into a scuffle with a Mosleyite with a National Service haircut and army-style shirt. They were separated by their friends, but not before Simon had managed to get in two or three winding punches. The fight elated him, releasing all the pent-up aggressions that banner-waving and slogan-shouting had merely stimulated. The meeting was now breaking up, and somehow he got separated from his friends. But there was a group from London University congregated around the Edith Cavell statue, and somehow he joined up with them, and they all went to a narrow, dark little pub up St Martin's Lane, where Simon downed three beers. Then they went to another in Cambridge Circus, where he downed two more.

It was when he left there that he was rolled. Walking blearily in the direction, he hoped, of the Leicester Square tube station, he passed into an arcade and ran straight into four or five of the Mosleyites he had tangled with earlier. They were quicker, and soberer, than he was. He felt the kick in his groin, and lunged out confusedly; then he felt fists in his eye, blows to the head, and then very little for the rest of the two or three minutes they used to do him over. When he came to, five minutes later, he was set up like a Guy Fawkes dummy against the doorway of a second-hand bookseller's. His nose was bleeding, his shirt and jacket were torn, and his wallet was gone.

Simon felt terrible, but—oddly—he also felt sober. He groped around him, groggily tried his feet. Soon he would be able to stand. He patted the inside pocket of his jacket. No wallet. He put his hand gingerly round to the back pocket of his flannels. A threepenny bit. Merely opening his eyes was painful. He groped blindly around the paved floor of the arcade again. No wallet. No money. He felt in the top pocket of his sports jacket: thank God, his return ticket was still there. Simon had no idea, such was his inexperience, what he would have done without the stub of his train ticket. Now all he had to do was to get to Paddington.

It was the countryman's way to walk, and Simon walked. His eye was horribly swollen, but his legs held him up well. When he got into Leicester Square he found a young policeman and asked him the general direction of Paddington, braving his disapproving stare.

'Been in the wars, have you?' he was asked.

'It was the bloody Fascists,' said Simon.

'Yes, well, if you ask me you're two of a kind,' said the policeman. But he pointed out the way.

Set on the right course, Simon soon began noticing signs, and before long he was walking with more confidence, and in no great pain. He stopped at a public lavatory and cleaned himself up. With the buoyancy of youth, he suddenly felt full of life again. There was plenty of time before the last train to Oxford. He walked on and on, noticing everything with fresh curiosity. The pavements got harder and harder, but still, the distance presented no problems: he had often walked further with his adoptive father round the estate of Sir Henry Beesley. It was around ten o'clock when he came to the area called Paddington.

The feeling came to him slowly: first it was a faint sense of unease, a hollowness in the belly, and he attributed it to the beating-up he had suffered, to the pitch of excitement he had been screwed up to all day, to a lack of food and a surfeit of beer. To anything except the real thing. For this feeling, he realized, was not only hollow: it was eerie. Here was a succession of houses—grimy, early nineteenth-century houses—small hotels and lower middle-class homes. He had known areas like this before, if not around Yeasdon, then in Bristol and in Oxford: grimy, depressing areas that cling around railway stations are all very like each other. Mean, protective of privacy, without dignity, they seem to stretch endlessly forward, to create their own dingy infinity, even though you know that five minutes away there are streets, and lights, and shops. At the corners you turn, and see more of the same, and you feel enmeshed, caught in a maze.

And yet *here*, in *these* streets, among *these* houses, Simon seemed to have a clue to the maze. Here at this corner, for example ... if he were to turn here, to go down this street ...

Without so much as a glance at his watch, with the unwilled certainty of a sleepwalker, he turned and went down that street.

Broughton Street it said on the first house in the first terraced row. Simon knew the name, had heard it. And he knew that at the next corner he must cross the road, and then turn again. Into Farrow Street. That was it, Farrow Street. And Farrow Street would be more of the same: some narrow, late-Georgian houses, some low, mean dwellings built in the early days of the railway age. They would be

the same, but they would be different, because they would
be still more familiar: they would be *known*. And he would
come to No. 17, on the right, and he would know the tiny
patch of garden between the pavement and the house, know
the two off-white steps up to the front door, know the knocker
. . . What *was* that knocker like? Yes—a grinning gnome in
brass, set low down in the door, where a child could grasp
its fearful leer, his heart thumping the while, preferring it
to the more fearful alternative of remaining out on the street.

He crossed the road, turned again, and walked up Farrow
Street. He felt he knew every crack in the paving stones,
every railing and doorway. He recognized at once the squat
form of the house, his old home; knew again the pale yellow
roses in the scrap of garden—not very flourishing, and
coated with grime. Here were the steps, much dirtier than
when he'd climbed them, here was the knocker, which now
he had to bend down to touch. But the door was wrong. It
was now dark green. What had it been then? Brown. Dark
brown. But it was the same door. There was a crack down
the lower left-hand panel.

Simon took a few steps backward into the street, and
surveyed the house. Suddenly his arm had to lunge out and
clutch on to a lamp-post for support. He was possessed by two
contrary impulses—to go up and knock at the door, and to
run away and put the house behind him. 'Who am I?' asked
one voice. 'You are Simon Cutheridge,' answered a second.
There was no one in the street. Blinds were down, curtains
drawn, and behind them—mere shadows—figures moved
around in the dimly lit rooms. It was an atmosphere neither
attractive nor cosy, but it was not sinister, not threatening.
'What could you say, if you knocked at the door?' asked
his second voice. 'I could say I am . . . I could say I once
lived here,' came back the first. 'Once lived here, and . . .'

The voices stopped, and a sort of blankness seemed to
enter Simon's mind, penetrate its every corner.

And suddenly he was walking. Like a bolt from a bow he
was walking away, and then, though he was breathing

heavily, he broke into a run. He went not the way he came, but forward, on to the Station. He was getting away from there, getting out of the area. He knew the way to the Station. It would be over there. He turned—left, then left again, then right. Suddenly the lights were in front of him; he was leaving the insidious, mean streets, and was back on a highway, on a road of shops and cafés and pubs, back in the warm world, with everyday human traffic.

A corner pub had a piano playing inside, a Greek café sent warm smells wafting over the pavement, a prostitute smiled at him hopefully. He blinked, as if he had known this scene, but never like this. Had known it, but darker. He looked left, and there was Paddington Station, there was the station hotel. He had only to walk a hundred yards and cross the street and he would be there. He leaned for a moment against the wall of a shop, a poky little newsagent's. He had come through. He had got out. He had . . . he had *failed*. He had flunked it.

But his legs would not allow him to turn back again. He swallowed, took a breath, then walked down to the traffic lights and across the road. Within minutes the subdued late-night bustle of Paddington Station closed in on him. He looked at the placard with train departures on it, then ran to his platform. Outside the ticket gate there was a knot of his fellow protestors. Immediately he was in the middle of them, getting high again on indignation, feeling the exhilaration of political action, or what seemed very like it. They all had experiences to swap, things that had happened to them since they split up. Simon told of the London University students, the pubs he had drunk in, the beating up. He told them more sketchily about his walk to the Station. About his experience in Farrow Street he kept silent. How could it mean anything to anyone but him? And besides . . . that part of his life was secret.

As the train pulled out, and only then, he felt safe. Yet how could he account for that sour taste in his mouth, of failure and of guilt?

CHAPTER 3

Once Simon was back in Oxford, it was easy for him to let Farrow Street hide itself in a corner of his mind. The rest of his first term passed in a frenzy of activity. Political impulses still bore him on at a hectic rate, a senior member of his college was trying hard to seduce him, he had met a girl who interested him. He drank a lot of beer, went to the odd dance, even landed a small part in the college play. There were lectures and lab classes, and quite a bit of football in the afternoons. It wasn't necessary—it wasn't even easy—to think.

When he went back home to Yeasdon in December it was much more difficult to put the thought to one side. In fact the mere act of sitting on a little train without corridor that drew slowly into Yeasdon Station pricked the thought into tormenting life: as his heart knocked against his ribs, he knew it had knocked thus in nineteen forty-one. He was the same person, only now he was going home, and then he had been going into the unknown. Was that why his heart had knocked on that May day?

Outside the station the first person he saw—stretched out under a car, as he seemed to have been stretched since he was fourteen or fifteen years old—was his best friend in Yeasdon, Micky Malone.

'Hey, Oxford boy! Yer look as if yer'd seen a ghost!'

'Micky!'

Simon put his case down on the forecourt, and Micky scrambled out from under the car.

'What are you so bloody pale for? Don't they feed you there?'

'I suppose I have seen a ghost, like you said. I was just remembering in the train, how we all came down here for the first time.'

'Is that all? Can't remember a thing about it meself.'

'I do. Or at least I tell myself I do.'

'"The boy from nowhere",' said Micky, quoting a name the evacuee kids had given Simon at the time. 'Well, what's it like being at Oxford, then, boy?'

And they'd gone on to talk of other things.

Of course his mother (as he called her, without a trace of self-consciousness) realized quite early on in the vacation that Simon was unusually preoccupied, and she guessed that it wasn't the new experience of university that was making him so.

'Something's happened, hasn't it?' she asked him, on his second evening home.

'I suppose so,' said Simon. 'I was in London, and I saw the house where I used to live.'

Dot thought for a bit.

'And did you knock on the door?'

'No. I—I found I didn't want to.'

'Well, that's all right, then.'

She knew, of course, that it was not. Dot Cutheridge was in her way a clever woman. She made no attempt to tell him that past things were better not mulled over in that way. He would come out of it in his own time. There was a sort of serene confidence about Dot these days. When you have reared a child to the age of twenty, seen him launched into adult life, your task is in a sense done, your life has had its fulfilment. So, at any rate, Dot Cutheridge and many like her thought, then.

At that time of year there was not much to be done around Sir Henry Beesley's estate, otherwise Simon might have helped his father there, as he always had done during his summer holidays from school. There was as yet no great pressure of college work either. Simon took long, brisk winter walks, and on these walks his mind refused to stay empty for long. Simon struggled to remember.

He had told Micky that he remembered 'or at least I tell myself that I do.' And that was the problem, wasn't it? We

say we remember things, but after a time just the saying it
has created a static picture in our mind that stands in for
the real memory. But surely that wasn't so in this case?
He had almost never talked about his train journey from
Paddington to Yeasdon, had surely not thought about it for
years, not since the early days. Yet there the memory had
been: sitting on the train as it pulled into the station,
his heart thumping, the faces of the reception committee
standing on the platform, some sense of an ordeal, a challenge, ahead.

Then what else could he remember from that time?

He was conscious that for the first months at Yeasdon
he had had a nagging feeling of guilt at deceiving the
Cutheridges. *Could* a child that young feel guilt? Perhaps
that was his first dawning of a moral awareness. Foolish, of
course, to feel guilty now. What was done was surely done
on orders, or at least under influence too strong for a
mere child to resist. And he had half understood that the
Cutheridges had wanted to be deceived. But looking back
he could feel kinship with that guilty child—ingratiating
himself, deceiving, suffering guilt.

He was conscious too that at the time there were many
things he could have told the Cutheridges, could have told
Mr Thurston and all the people who tried to find out who
he was, but had deliberately not told them. Why had he
kept silent? There was some strong influence—he did not
know of what kind—from his former life telling him to:
telling him not to reveal who he was, where he came from,
how he had come to be on that train. But he felt there was
another reason too: from the first moment he had loved the
Cutheridges, had wanted to be with them, had opted for
them rather than what he had left. He had loved them even
as he deceived them.

What was it he could have told them, had he wished?

Simon was sitting on a tree stump on the edge of a little
coppice. He was wearing a heavy sweater that his mother
had knitted for him under a tweed sports jacket, but never-

theless he shivered. He gazed ahead of him, across the rolling fields towards Yeasdon. No—that was not the way to bring it back. He shut his eyes. At once he saw the door in Paddington—brown, with a split in the panel on the bottom left side, with the two steps up to it, and the sooty flowers to either side. Was this a memory of 1941, or of his experience earlier that year? Of 1941, surely. The door was brown, the panel was not seen from above.

What pictures came to him from behind that door?

He had no doubt that his mind had retained, for months or years after his arrival in Yeasdon, imprints of the reality behind that door, pictures of his first five years. Were they now entirely faded? He frowned. A figure. A large female figure in black . . . A man . . . something vaguely inimical about him, something hostile clinging to that vague impression . . . other shapes, mere outlines . . . all of them in the background, none of them attaining definition.

Nothing more. Nothing of any solidity at all. No faces topping the figures. Nothing.

'I am Simon Cutheridge,' he said to himself on his walk home. 'You are also a boy who once lived at 17, Farrow Street,' said that irritating voice, in counterpoint inside his head. 'He isn't Simon Cutheridge. He isn't Simon Thorn either. Don't you even want to know his name?'

Simon's best friend in Yeasdon was Micky Malone. Many people in the village found this odd. Micky had never had the slightest interest in anything academic. He could read well enough, but his writing was atrocious. He had always had a passion for bikes and cars, and had been destined as sure as God made apples to be a garage mechanic, which was what he now was. Micky was genial, a humorist, and dubiously honest. He was stocky and pug-faced, where Simon had a sort of adolescent elegance and a long face that was not handsome, but gave promise of distinction. Micky was direct and outgoing, where Simon used politeness and manner as a guard. The boys from Yeasdon who had passed the eleven-plus had gone on to the Buckridge Grammar

School, and had kept themselves rather aloof from those
who had failed it and had gone on to the little secondary
school in Yeasdon. Yet, in spite of all this, Simon's best
friend had been Micky Malone, idling away the years before
he could leave school at fourteen, grasping joyously at the
opportunities for easy pleasures in the years since then.

Presumably the reason was that Micky had also been an
evacuee. All the other children—some very soon, some at
the end of the war—had gone home, but not Micky or
Simon. After Micky had come to Yeasdon his mother had
paid him one visit, in 1943. She wore her hair in a headscarf,
swore like a trooper, and within ten minutes of her arrival
demanded to know where the bookmaker's was. When the
war ended nothing was heard of her. Micky's adoptive
mother hoped she'd gone off with a Yank, though that
seemed rather a poor return for helping us to save the free
world. Anyway, Micky stayed on, and was welcome to, for
he'd been part of the family from the first hour. He never,
though, became entirely Yeasdon: there was always something indefinably cockney settled there as a bedrock under
the veneer of West Country ways. Even his speech retained
traces of its East End flavour. He was a cockney at heart,
the Yeasdon people said, especially when he had just pulled
a fast one on them.

During the Christmas vacation Simon and Micky went
around a lot, as they always had. Both of them were ardent
and undiscriminating cinema-goers (it wasn't so long since
Simon had stopped calling himself a film fan). They went
to the Odeon and the ABC in Buckridge once a week; they
went for a drink, sometimes in Yeasdon, sometimes further
afield; they went to dances, and sometimes on Micky's
afternoon off they did a coffee-bar crawl around Buckridge.
It was their last spell of really close friendship: by Easter
both of them would have a regular girlfriend. For these five
weeks they were so close it was a foregone conclusion that
Micky would pretty soon find out what was on Simon's
mind.

'I don't know why you're botherin',' he said one day, as they sat in the Boccaccio Coffee Lounge and sipped the creamy foam from the tops of their cappucini. 'It's the same wiv me, isn't it? I could go back to 'Ackney, find out where I come from, find out what happened to me Ma, as if I cared. I wouldn't be so flamin' daft. Waste o' bleedin' time.'

'It's not the same,' insisted Simon. The coffee-machine hissed menacingly in the background like a horror-film snake as he tried to put it into words. 'First of all, you know you're Michael Malone. You had a dad called Malone.'

'You seem to know more than I do, mate. I don't remember no dad.'

'All right, you had a mother called Malone.'

'Right old cow she was, an' all.'

'But still, you had one. She gave you her name, she came here, people saw her. You came from an actual address in Hackney, you're on record as having been to one of the schools there.'

'What's that supposed to mean? I expect you went to one too.'

'OK, but there's no record of it. I don't exist on paper before 1941; I have no history before I stepped on to the platform of the station here. I haven't got parents, not real ones, and I haven't got a name.'

'You said you were called Simon Thorn.'

'I think I made that up.'

'Cunning little bugger! Couldn't ha' been more'n six.'

'I don't know how old I was. Don't know how old I am, come to that. We always celebrated the day I got here as my birthday—we said I was five on that day.'

Simon looked down into the white and brown dregs of his coffee, thinking hard. Micky shifted on his stool in embarrassment: Micky didn't like having to be serious for any length of time.

'I think,' said Simon at last, 'I think I made up that name because it had been drummed into me that I wasn't to tell anyone my real name. Or where I came from, or anything about myself. I think I told lies—partly because I'd been told to, but partly because I wanted to stay here, wanted to be accepted by Mum and Dad—by the Cutheridges. I think all those first months after I arrived I was playing a part . . . until the part fitted, became natural: I *was* the part. And quite soon I forgot all that had gone before.'

'You'd remember yer own name, surely.'

'I don't, though. I was only five or so. Perhaps if I heard it . . . '

'Do you remember getting on the train in London?'

'No. I found I knew the way from . . . from my home to Paddington. It wasn't far, but I knew it—just instinctively took the right way. But I don't remember getting on the train. Do you?'

'I tell you, I don't remember a thing about that time. I was only five too. And I don't go grubbing around in my memory—too much going on now, this moment, to bother wi' bleedin' past 'istory. I do know you joined the gang last of all.'

'What do you mean? You *do* remember!'

'No, I don't. But you remember Nellie Tucker?'

'I *think* so. Wasn't she—?'

'One of us. Yeah. Anyway, she came down, must be a couple o' months ago, to visit old Mrs Potter, who'd looked after her. Proper little London sparrow she is—bit of all right, too. Shop assistant. Anyway, we went out a couple o' times while she was here. Bit different from these country girls. She—'

'Yes?'

'She let me go the whole way, first time of askin'.'

Micky's face took on a drooling grin of reminiscence.

'I don't want all the sexy details. What did she say about *me*?'

'Oh yes, well—she's got this marvellous memory, see? Sort of photographic, only not for words, more for pictures, like. Well, naturally we got talkin' about how we come 'ere. The evacuation, an' that. And o' course we got talkin' about you. And Nellie's got this picture in her mind: us all in a group, like, wi' the teacher checkin' up on our names. Then the teacher got on the train to sort out which was to go in which compartments, and she's got this picture o' you walkin' up the platform wi' a satchel over your shoulder, just joinin' up wi' the group, and gettin' on the train with us.'

Simon sat there, considering. Nellie's picture called up no memories.

'Case,' he said. 'I had a case, not a satchel. I've still got it.'

'That's right. She said you had a case in your hand, and a little satchel over your shoulder.'

'I think she's wrong. I'd still have had it when I got here, and I know I didn't.'

'Little kids goin' to school often did have satchels. Wi' their names on in indelible ink, case they got lost.'

There came to Simon, he did not know from where, a sharp image of a leather bag, thrown from a window, sailing through the air, to land on a grassy bank.

' 'Ere,' said Micky, who had been thinking, and had got really interested for the first time: 'perhaps you threw it away when you realized it had your name on it.'

'Perhaps I did,' said Simon.

'Cunning little bugger!' said Micky again. He'd never before imagined that Simon might be endowed with that cunning that he saw as his own birthright. 'You never know, perhaps things will come back to you. They do sometimes, you know.'

'I know. I think something just did. But it's more likely the opposite will happen, isn't it?'

'What? You'll forget?'

'Yes. And think I remember things I don't really remember. What I ought to do is write down everything I remember *now*. And if anything comes back to you—'

'It won't mate. I live in the present. Why don't you try it?'

Simon did write down what he remembered, in a stiff-backed exercise book which he was to keep and add to for many years. He tried to be scrupulously honest, marking specially the things he was dubious about. When, on the last day of the vacation, he read over all he had written, he saw clearly that it didn't amount to much.

By then he had something else to occupy his mind. Early in January Tom Cutheridge received a blow on the head from the hoof of an estate horse. He lay dangerously ill in Buckridge Hospital for ten days, and Simon and his mother waited and watched and comforted each other. In those days, before Tom was out of danger, Simon was closer to his mother than he had ever been. I belong to them, he thought; only to them. Thinking it over, his concern over his lost, forgotten first years took the shape of a sort of disloyalty. As he sat by the bed, or in the dreary hospital waiting-room, it became something he was ashamed of. Having felt guilty of funking the challenge of 17 Farrow Street, Simon now felt guilty about even wanting to know the truth about his origins.

Perhaps that over-developed capacity for guilt was in itself a clue to his past.

CHAPTER 4

Though Simon Cutheridge went often enough through Paddington Station in the years that followed, he did not return to the Paddington area, or to the house that he knew had once been his home, until the spring of 1964. This was shortly after the break-up of his marriage.

The marriage had been one of these modern affairs where the two partners believe they know everything there is to know about the other before they get to the altar or the Registrar's desk, and find out soon after that they don't. Simon had met Ruth, his wife, in his last year at

Oxford, had lived with her off and on during his Research
Studentship at Leeds. Then they had got married, and
things had begun almost at once to go wrong. The baby
girl that was born did not perform that miracle of
cementing the marriage which is so often expected of
babies. When she died of pneumonia at ten months
the marriage headed rapidly for collapse. The random
acrimony and the flare-ups into full-scale rows were now
unalleviated by any warmth of reconciliation. 'You're just
not *here* half the time,' Ruth had said, during one of the
bitterest of their rows. 'Perhaps it's because you don't
know who you are.' Both of them soon realized it could
only end one way. Simon took the Tom Lehrer records
and the Beechams, Ruth—the Beatles and the Karajans,
and they split up without regrets, and almost without
rancour. I was spoilt by the Cutheridges, thought Simon
wearily. I'll never think relationships are easy again.

In spite of the ease and friendliness of the break, and in
spite of the insouciance with which liberated young people
at the time were supposed to regard a marriage break-up,
it was a shattering experience for Simon. It somehow seemed
a betrayal of all those years of warmth and fortressed domes-
ticity at Yeasdon. His first instinct was to get away from the
town, the job he associated with his marriage, and the
friends who had watched it empty itself of meaning month
by month. He applied for a position on the staff of the
London Zoo.

The governors and officials at the Zoo were cautious,
conservative and thorough: new members of their scientific
staff were not engaged lightly. Four of the best applicants
had their fares paid to London, with two nights at a
hotel, so that they could be seen, sized up, and interviewed
to the point of grilling. Their suitability (though this was
never put into words) had to be established from a social
and personal point of view, as well as from a scientific
one. On the afternoon of the second day Simon was given
a strong hint that the job was his if he wanted it.

The first thing he did was to ring his mother and father. 'I'll be able to get down more now,' he said.

'It's about time something good happened to you,' said his mother. 'Perhaps you're in for a lucky spell now.'

Simon had thought of the move to London more in the light of a clean break than as the beginning of a run of luck. But his mother—was it the remnant of some peasant superstition?—believed that luck, good and bad, went in cycles, and nothing in Simon's life so far had contradicted that belief. When he had rung off, he had to decide what to do with his evening.

He could hardly celebrate in any obvious fashion, even had he a mind to. He was in the same hotel as the three other applicants interviewed, and the broad hint had been given him under a vow of discretion. Keeping up a false front over drinks or dinner would be no fun at all. Simon decided to shower and change, and then give the others the slip, leave the hotel, and find what his mother would call a 'show' to go to.

His hotel was a modest but respectable one on the fringes of Bloomsbury, and when he left it he directed himself towards the theatres. An evening paper told him that *The Sound of Music* was still spreading cow-bells and schmaltz over Cambridge Circus, but there was Edith Evans in *Hay Fever* at the National, and an interesting new play called *Entertaining Mr Sloane* at the Arts. He'd find something, just by walking.

But he never reached the theatres at all. He was idling along New Oxford Street when, above the traffic noise, he heard raised voices. He halted in his tracks, looked down a murky passageway, and saw that he was near one of those dingy, down-at-heel blocks of municipal flats that still cling on in parts of central London, hiding shamefacedly behind the plate-glass shop-fronts like poor relations at a posh wedding. Suddenly, into the meagre courtyard at the end of the passage, there burst first a screaming woman, then, following her, a hefty, red-faced man bellowing abuse. She had not gone more than a few feet towards the street when he caught her. He pulled her round to face him, and began belabouring her about the head with heavy fists, punctuating the blows with all the words of sexual abuse that his sodden brain could dredge up.

'Here! Stop that!' began Simon. He started towards them, but almost at once the blows and the screams sent over him a wave—of recollection, of nausea, of fear, whatever it might be—that seemed to submerge him, that sent his legs staggering under him, so that he could only stop and clutch at the walls of the passageway for support. The voice continued to bellow insults, the fists to fall, but Simon could only cling there, his eyes closed, his stomach rising in great heaves of panic and remembered fear.

Suddenly windows opened above the dirty courtyard. Voices began to be raised in protest. One woman screamed: 'I've called the police.' The man straightened up, bellowed back an obscenity, and in a moment was barging past Simon, down the passage, and out into the street.

Gradually the panic subsided. He shook himself and opened his eyes, feeling very much less than heroic. He walked over to the sobbing bundle of clothes on the paved floor of the courtyard.

'Are you all right?'

'Oh, go to hell.'

An overpowering smell of sweat, urine and cheap spirits rose up and over him from the sobbing heap.

'You really ought to see a doctor, you know.'

'Oh, f—off.'

'Don't bovver abaht 'er, mate,' said a voice from the window above. 'It ain't the first time.'

'Enjoys it, if you ask me,' said a woman's voice.

'You might as well save yer breath,' said another. 'You'll get no thanks from 'er, I can tell you.'

So Simon, awkwardly and unhappily, turned on his heels and slunk away. Out into New Oxford Street, along to the tube at Tottenham Court Road, then down into its depths, where he bought a ticket for Paddington.

When he emerged from the station he made his way, straight, confident, unflinching, to Farrow Street. He knew the way. Suddenly it occurred to him that he knew the way *from* Farrow Street *to* the Station. That was the way he had done it—or had done it as Simon Cutheridge. But he seemed to know the reverse journey equally well. How often had he done it as—as whatever his name was then?

As he walked, he asked himself why he had come back. Because he had just funked intervening in a fight, and had by some quirky idea of compensation determined to follow through what he had funked eight years ago? But he had been in fights before, and had not funked them: playground fights, the brush with the Fascists, an after-hours pub brawl in Leeds. What had been crucial here had been the *domestic* violence, the man and woman fighting. Had he funked it, or had it dredged from the silt of his early memories . . . *something*?

He walked on, a tallish man in a not very fashionable sports jacket, good-looking in a not-too-obvious, English way, a way that had been more admired in the 'fifties than it was in the 'sixties. Fair-haired, engaging, but somehow reserved, with the beginnings of lines of care along the high forehead and from the corners of his eyes. A fresh, well-meaning, slightly troubled boy-man.

That was what the woman saw when she opened the door of No. 17. He had gone up to the house confidently, walked up the steps, knocked without hesitation on the door, and then waited.

'Coming! Won't be a mo! Just got to put me frock on!' came a voice. It was a voice that wakened no memories. Simon's stomach remained stable. When the woman opened the door it was obvious she had been dressing after a bath. There was a smell of talcum, and her dress hung loosely on her substantial body, and was not done up at the back. Suddenly, but not for that reason, Simon felt awkward.

'Yes?'

'I'm sorry—this is going to sound rather funny—'

'Won't be the first time I've heard funny things at my own front door,' said the woman, her sharp, ironic face surveying him coolly. 'It's not religious, is it?'

'No, it's not religious.'

'Because they can be a bit over the top, in my experience. Oh, and by the way, I don't ever buy things at the door.'

'It's not that either. You see, I used to live here . . . '

'Oh yes?' The woman was polite, not specially interested. A house, for a Londoner, is usually no more than a machine for living in, not a respository for sentimental memories.

'It was a long time ago, at the beginning of the war.'

'You wouldn't have been more than a nipper then.'

'That's right. The point is, I wondered . . . Have you lived here long?'

'Matter of five years. Bit of a draught-trap, and bigger than we need, but we've got Bert's parents living with us, and it means we can keep out of each other's way.'

'Do you remember who you bought it from?'

'People called Ponting.'

'Had they lived here long?'

'Only three or four years, as I remember. They retired to the coast somewhere. Why?'

'Well . . . ' Simon's face had fallen with disappointment, but he began to improvise a story. 'You see, my parents were killed in the war, and I lost touch with my relations.'

'Oh, really?' The story made him human, interested her distantly, as something she might read in the *Sunday Pictorial* would. 'You wanted to find someone who knew them, did you? Really, I don't know . . . '

'I wonder whether the neighbours . . . '

'On that side it's Pakis. They'd be no use, because we didn't *have* Pakis then, did we? Not *here*. On the other side there's people I don't know, but they moved in after us. Have you tried the pub?'

'No. Do you think they'd know anything there?'

'Pubs are always good places to go to with something like that. Then even if you don't get what you want you can always have a drop of something so you haven't wasted your time.' She laughed with the rich laugh of someone who's had a drop or two in her time. 'It's the Fox and Newt, down the end of the road. Arnold Stebbings has been there an age, I do know that, so you could do worse than try him.'

'I'll do that,' said Simon. 'Many thanks.'

'Don't mention it. Sorry I couldn't be more help,' said the woman, with that uninvolved friendliness the English rather go in for.

Why didn't I ask to see the house? Simon asked himself as he walked down the road in the direction she had pointed out. Too embarrassed. And it wouldn't have told me anything. Everything would have changed inside. They'd have taken their furniture—*them*, my family. Unless—you never knew—the wallpaper in one of the rooms had been the same . . . But how would I have explained why I wanted to see it?

Certainly the Fox and Newt aroused no memories, but then: how could it? It was a steamy, varnish-and-brass suburban London pub, but he could never have seen the inside of it. It was still early in the evening, and possible to have the landlord to himself for five minutes' conversation.

'Oh aye, I've been here a while,' said Arnold Stebbings, polishing glasses, 'but not *that* long. Only since 'forty-nine. Not before the war. I was *in* the war, my lad, and I only came to London on my demob.'

'Hell!' said Simon, drinking into his pint disappointedly. 'What was it you wanted?'

'You see, I lost both my parents in the war.' (Suddenly there came, unbidden, to Simon's mind that line from *The Importance of Being Earnest:* 'It would be nearer the truth to say that my parents seem to have lost me . . . '). 'I was . . . adopted. And I wondered if there was anybody still living around here who . . . would remember me. And them.'

It would do, as a story. It was getting better. The landlord, anyway, was displaying that non-committal but friendly interest.

'Let's see now. There's been a deal of changes, I can tell you. Well—Paddington's not really a place where people settle down, is it? There's still some of the old 'uns around, though. Jessie Pyke, but she's senile, more or less, so I wouldn't . . . Jack Watkyns! That's the chap for you!'

'Where does he live?'

'He's a regular here. What's today? Wednesday. He wouldn't thank you for disturbing him during *Coronation Street,* but he'll be in here directly afterwards. Have you got the price of a pint for him?'

'Yes, of course.'

'Well, you settle Jack down at a table with a pint he hasn't had to pay for, and he'll tell you all he knows. And he's a straight bloke: he won't make up what he doesn't remember.'

So when the torrid doings of the young Elsie Tanner were over for the night, Simon was introduced to old Jack Watkyns. He bought him a pint, took him over to a table, and let him tell all he knew. He was a fat, none-too-clean old man, probably around his mid-sixties, and he'd lived just round the corner from Farrow Street all his life. What he didn't know about the inhabitants he had been prevented from knowing by the inbuilt privacy-mania of Londoners, not from any lack of will to find out.

'You say you used to live here? As a boy, was it? Now, which number in Farrow Street would that be?'

'Number seventeen. It's got a green front door now, but it was brown then, and there's yellow roses in the garden.'

'Got it. Three up from the shop. You're right, that front door did used to be brown. So this was wartime, was it?'

'Yes. The beginning of the war.'

'So that would be when the Simmeters were there, then—they'd be your people, would they? I remember there were children.'

The surname aroused the faintest of echoes in Simon's mind.

'Do you remember much about them?'

'But you won't need to ask me, young man, if they're your folks.'

'We got separated . . . I think they were killed.'

'Ah!' said Jack Watkyns, pulling deeply on his pint, and clearly wondering if there was likely to be any follow-up. 'Could be. They moved, I remember that. They were here for years and years, but they moved early in the war . . . Was it northwards?'

'Northwards? Like Yorkshire, you mean?'

'No—Kilburn, Edgware, somewhere like that. Wait, though: I've an idea it was Islington, not the north at all. Anyway, never heard of them after that. Not that I had much to do with them while they were here.'

'You didn't know them well?'

'No. Private lot, so far as I remember. No disrespect, but they kept themselves very much to themselves—that kind of folks. Church, too, I reckon. I never saw him in here that I remember.'

'Who was *he*, then?' Simon felt his heart beating faster.

'That was the son. Let's see, what was his name? Lawrence? Lionel? Leonard. Leonard Simmeter, maybe. Sounds about right. Could be I never heard it, though.'

The name aroused no response in Simon. But if it was his father, he would always have known him as Daddy, presumably.

'Was it a large family?'

'Fairly so, as families go *these* days. And all crammed in together there.'

'Who actually was there in the family?'

'Oh, my God, it's a long time ago. You're asking a lot, young fellow. Yes, I will have another, since you're so kind . . . Thanks. Pulls a good pint, does Arnold. Well now, I can remember Mother. Big woman of fifty-odd then. Widow lady. Then there were three or four children. This Lawrence or Lionel or Leonard. And his wife—pale little body. And his sister—about the same age, or perhaps a bit younger. Good-looking girl. And . . . oh dear . . . I *think* there may have been a younger brother. Don't know that I could put a name to him—Ernie, could it be?—but I seem to recall a lad in RAF uniform. This Len—I'm sure it was Len, now I come to say the name—he worked at Paddington Station, that I do know. In the ticket office. I had a spell as a porter, so I'm pretty sure of that. But more I can't call to mind.'

'It's a lot. I'm very grateful.'

'You say they were killed?'

'Yes . . . I think so.'

'You don't seem too sure, lad. That's a bit queer, isn't it? You wouldn't be looking to find relatives, would you, young feller?'

'Well—something like that.'

'I never knew folks as was happier for finding relatives. Y'know, lad, if they didn't care for you then, they're not going to care about you now.'

'I know,' said Simon, getting up abruptly. 'Silly, isn't it?'

But when he got back to his hotel room that night, the first thing he did was to take up the last volume of the London Telephone Directory. There were four entries under Simmeter:

Simmeter, E., 16 Leith Grove, SE5.
Simmeter L. J., 25 Miswell Tce, EC1.
Simmeter and Fox, TV Repairs, 76 High St, SE6.
Simmeter W., 7 Burdett St, NW3.

He looked under Simmetter, Simeter, even Scimeter, but he found no more entries.

He took out his pocket book and pencil, and noted down the details of the four.

CHAPTER 5

Next morning, over scrambled eggs and toast and marmalade, Simon propped his pocket book up against the teapot and contemplated the entries. Thank God it was an unusual name, he said to himself.

It was fairly clear where he ought to start—supposing, that is, he decided to start at all. NW3 was Hampstead, that he did know, because his professor at Leeds had moved there when he got a job at London University. He had as yet no clear picture in his mind of the Simmeter family of Paddington, but Hampstead seemed an unlikely locality for them to rise to. In any case, the L. Simmeter was a much better bet. Jack Watkyns had mentioned Islington as a possibility. Simon turned to the theatre column in that morning's *Guardian*. Sadler's Wells Theatre, he knew, was in Islington. It was listed as EC1. Simon took it as his working hypothesis that Leonard or Lionel Simmeter had moved to Islington, where he had remained, while possibly his brother had eventually moved out to SE5. But his imagination had fixed on Simmeter, L. It was with him that Simon felt his mission lay.

Somehow by the end of breakfast there was no question that the mission would be undertaken.

Simon did not do anything about it at once. He took his suitcase along to King's Cross, and put it in the Left Luggage. He had an appointment at the Zoo for 11.15, and he took the tube to Baker Street. In the administrative offices that straddle the Zoo he was told that he would in the next day or two get a letter offering him the appointment. It was his if he wanted it.

'And we very much hope that you *do* want it,' said the Head of the Scientific Staff.

'Thank you,' said Simon. 'I think I do.'

'Marvellous. Delighted all this grilling hasn't put you off. You'll have three months' notice to give, I imagine, but with the summer vacation coming up, that might shorten it, perhaps? See what they say. We can be in touch as soon as we know when you can take up the appointment. We might be able to help you get somewhere to live.'

'That's kind of you,' said Simon. 'But just possibly I may be able to get something for myself. I have relatives . . . '

Before he left the administrative block at the Zoo, he asked if he might use a telephone. It would sound better, he thought, if the call did not come from a call box. He decided to assume a slight accent, so that if this attempt aborted and he had to find some alternative way of approaching them, his voice would not be recognized. Some instinctive caution told him not to broaden his natural West Country burr. He assumed the accent he knew well from his last few years: that of Leeds.

'Islington 4565,' came a voice at the other end, after he had let it ring five or six times. It was an old voice, a woman's voice, and it had once been a powerful mezzo—not a voice for telling good tidings to Zion, but one for launching Verdian imprecations. Now it was muffled and cracked by age.

'Good morning, I'm sorry to bother you, but I heard you might have a room to let.'

'Oh,' said the voice. There was a silence while she pondered. 'Well, I don't know . . . Mr Blore has been saying he might be moving soon, but he hasn't given notice.'

Spot on! said Simon to himself. First time! They do let rooms.

'It must be Mr Blore I heard it from,' he said. 'At a party. I shan't be wanting the room while summer' (he brought out this Leedsism with a sort of bravado) 'but it would be very convenient if I knew it would be waiting for me when I move down.'

'Well, as I say, he's not given his notice,' said the voice—hesitant, but as if hesitancy was not her natural mode. 'If he's leaving now he'll have to pay us two weeks' rent. That's in the agreement.'

'If he did leave before I was ready to take over the room, I'd be willing to pay from the time he left.'

'Oh . . . well, that's fair,' said the voice. It was the tone of one who called 'fair' anything advantageous to herself. But he seemed to have kindled sparks of interest. She added: 'Of course, we'd want to *see* you.'

It was a reasonable enough request, and just what Simon wanted, but the tone in which she said it was unendearing. There were plenty of Leeds landladies, Simon knew, who wanted to *see* their potential student lodger, but had unaccountably let the room already when they opened the door and found he was black. Was this the reason now, or would he have to present proof that he was house-trained, Christian, or non-smoker or drinker? The whimsical requirements of landladies could be legion.

'Yes, of course,' he said, in his most boyishly ingratiating tones. 'It would be quite easy for me to come round.'

'Provided it's clear I'm making no promises,' said the voice, with a nagging, grudging insistence. 'Would fiveish suit you? Then Len would be home.'

'That's fine,' said Simon. 'Fiveish it is.'

When he put the phone down he felt very pleased with himself, and nervously excited. He had another brisk walk around the Zoo, struck up a friendship with the squirrel monkeys which was to last all his working life, and ate a goodish lunch at the Restaurant. But by three he could contain his impatience no longer. He walked along Albany Street to the Regent's Park tube, and took a ticket to the Angel, Islington.

He had his Geographers' London with him, and he purposely avoided Miswell Terrace. He did not want to be seen hanging around before his appointment, and the form behind that voice on the phone could well be a peerer, a discreet puller-apart of lace curtains. He walked instead around every other street in the vicinity. Most of them were

rows of terraced houses, built early in the last century. They
were not unattractive, but their neglected state made them
appear skimpy and mean. Many were down at heel, some
derelict, and there lay over the district a miasma of half-
heartedness, littleness, failure. The unlovely council flats
were better: jollier, more open. In one of the streets there
was a cheerful, dirty collection of market barrows, with
friendly, untrustworthy sellers. He lingered round Sadler's
Wells. Elizabeth Fretwell in *The Girl of the Golden West*. No
time for that tonight: he would get the 8.50 train back to
Leeds. He turned away from the posters and went back to
the dingy streets of terraced houses. Really, though they
once had greater pretensions, now their effect was not unlike
Farrow Street, Paddington. The Simmeters, presumably,
had moved sideways, rather than up or down. What, he
wondered, had made them move at all?

At a quarter to five he stood at the end of Miswell Terrace.
One more of what he already had seen many of. He could
see No. 25: as dank and dejected as the rest. At ten to five
he was ringing on its doorbell.

Just when he was considering ringing again, a door
opened somewhere inside the house, and light penetrated
the mottled glass of the front door. He heard heavy footsteps, saw a looming shadow on the other side of the glass.
Two locks were turned, and then the door was opened.

She was a heavy old woman, in a shapeless black woollen
dress, with a plum-coloured cardigan over it, and slippers
on her feet. She was now fat, but Simon guessed she must
once have been a fine figure of a woman, in a massive kind
of way. Her cheeks were now round, and there were rolls of
fat around her neck, but the impression she gave was not
comfortable. The mouth was hard, the eyes calculating, and
behind all the flabbiness Simon sensed a lifetime of grim
purpose and iron will.

'So you've come,' she announced.

She squeezed her mouth into no similitude of a smile, but
from the way she stood regarding him, right hand on hip,

Simon could have sworn he sensed a silent satisfaction that he was white.

'Yes, I've come.'

'What's your name, then?'

He smiled, and watched her as he said: 'Simon Cutheridge.'

No flicker passed across that hard face. Simon felt sure that the name meant nothing to her.

'And where are you from?'

'Leeds,' said Simon. He had already decided that for the moment he would say nothing of Yeasdon.

'Could hear it was the North somewhere,' said the old woman, with a trace of contempt she took no trouble to disguise. It's common knowledge, her manner seemed to say, that Northerners are inferior: if *I* think so, it's common sense, and *everybody* thinks so. 'You'd better come in. Though really, I don't know ... Mr Blore's said nothing to me about leaving, not immediately. Nor to Len either, because I asked him at dinner-time.'

'If I could just leave you my address and telephone number in Leeds, so that if he does leave you could contact me. It would save you the expense of advertising.'

'It would do that, I suppose,' she said, with that same grudging tone she had used throughout, but with a tiny sparkle in her eye. 'Well, you'd better see the room.'

That was more than Simon had dared to hope. She switched on a light—a dim bulb behind a basic shade, that gave a dubious illumination to hall and stairway. Both had been redecorated in the last year or two, with a miserable cheap wallpaper with a tiny pattern of brown leaves. It had left it indescribably cheerless. The old woman cared nothing about his impressions of the place. She turned and began labouring up the stairs.

'It's a nice room, very nice,' she said, as she paused for breath on the first landing. 'There's everything there, all nice and convenient. And a gas ring ... '

She began again, heaving her bulk towards the top floor,

jangling her keys as if she were a wardress. Simon made a
mental note not to leave anything of a personal nature in
his room, if it ever became his. At the top landing the woman
turned on another dim light—this time a bare bulb. There
were two rooms on this floor, both of them with Yale locks
fitted. The woman pondered over her keys, selected one,
then opened the door of the room straight ahead.

The bedsitter thus revealed was small, and predictably
depressing. There was a sofa-bed against one wall, and an
old, re-covered armchair drawn up to a gas fire. On a
laminated shelf by the mantelpiece was the gas ring that
was apparently one of the attractions of the place. Under
the window, curtained with dirty lace, was an infirm wooden
table with an aluminium and plastic chair pulled up to it.
The only signs of life and individuality were the mug and
dirty plate on the table, the assorted paperbacks scattered
around, a copy of *Playboy*, and the pictures which had been
pinned to the walls—a large Lowry, a Labour Party poster,
and a girlie calendar.

'Yes, well it looks very . . . nice,' said Simon.

The woman sniffed, and looked venomously around the
walls.

'*He* put those up.'

'It's just what I need—really. I'm grateful to you for
showing it to me.'

'Don't mention it,' muttered the woman, in her tight-
lipped way.

'If I could perhaps pay some kind of deposit . . . '

'Well, I don't know about that. Seeing as how we aren't
sure as Mr Blore is leaving. I don't know what would be
right . . . Oh, that's Len now. He'll know. You'd better talk
to him about it.'

From two flights down Simon had heard the sound of a
key in the door, and the door opening. He mentally noted
that the old woman's hearing was unimpaired. She ushered
him out, closed up the room, and began labouring down the
stairs, clutching hard at the banisters and breathing heavily.

Simon followed her down, his heart beating. When she had regained the hall, she turned to a door which divided the family's living quarters from the rest of the house. She called:

'Len!'

The man who came to the door and faced them across the little hallway was fairly tall—perhaps close on six feet—with square shoulders. But his chest was hollow, his frame bony, his face sunken, and he gave an impression of meagreness, of having aged prematurely. He wore a fawn cardigan, buttoned around his stomach, and he was clutching an evening paper. What struck Simon was his manner: under a hearty exterior he seemed unaccountably nervous, and he rubbed his hands together a good deal, perhaps because when he did not they tended to flutter. He greeted Simon with an ingratiating eagerness which, in its effect, was the reverse of welcoming.

'Ah—you're the young man. Nice to meet you. Well—that's very satisfactory!'

He had closed the door to the family quarters, and when they had shaken hands they stood in the cramped little hallway. Obviously it was not going to be easy to gain admittance to the inner sanctum of the Simmeter family life. The old woman was looking at Len, behaving towards him in a way that Simon found hard to comprehend, as it seemed a compound of opposites—both commanding, yet almost fawning, strong-minded yet nervous and uncertain. Had the relationship changed as she had grown older and feebler? Had she once ruled with an iron hand, and now was uncertain of her power?

'He wants to pay a deposit,' said the old woman, looking at Len.

Len Simmeter's manner became still more friendly, without the slightest degree of warmth behind it.

'I don't see why not, Ma. That's very generous of him.'

'Not at all,' said Simon. 'I thought that if Mr Blore *did*

give notice in the next three months, then I'd have the right to the room.'

'And so you would,' said Len. 'Quite so. And we'd return it to you if he stayed put. Naturally. Very fair arrangement all round. You told him the rent for the room, Mother?'

'No, I didn't.' Again she looked at him, covertly, uncertain whether she had done right or wrong. She seemed to have done right.

'Well,' said Len Simmiter, rubbing his hands, 'it's four pounds ten a week—' It was, for those times, decidedly steep. But Len had left his voice on a rising intonation, so that if Simon protested he could add: 'but for you we'll say four pounds.' However, Simon had made up his mind, and he quickly accepted.

'That seems very reasonable,' he said, with a naive smile. 'I know that things down here cost that bit more than they do up north.'

'Quite. You've no idea—what with the rates, and overheads, and everything. This lot we've got lording it at the LCC at the moment don't help matters either. What they're not willing to do with other people's money! You're like pigs in clover up north, so I've heard, where prices are concerned!' He was protesting too much, and he pulled himself up short. 'Moving south, eh? Got a good job down here, then, have you?'

'I'm going to be working at the London Zoo. On the scientific staff there.'

'Nice! Very good! Work with a bit of class—professional, like. Well, young feller-me-lad, if you'd like to leave your name and address, and this deposit you mentioned, we can be in touch as soon as things sort themselves out at this end.'

Simon tore a piece of paper from his pocket book, and wrote on it against the wall his name, address, and telephone number. He registered with satisfaction that the name seemed to mean nothing to Len either. Then he took from his wallet two five-pound notes. Len Simmeter, who had been standing by rubbing his hands, took them from him, just a shade too hurriedly.

'That's handsome of you,' he said. 'Nice to do business with a real gentleman. I really hope something turns up here. There's Miss Cosgrove in the other room, of course, but there's no hope that she'll move on. Made herself very comfortable here, she has—*oh* yes! But I think you'll find a room waiting for you, when you want to move down. When was it, did you say?'

'June,' said Simon. 'I imagine it'll be towards the end of June.'

'Good, good,' said the man, opening the door to show that the interview was at an end. 'Well, we'll be in touch. And we'll hope to see you down here in June.'

'Thank you very much,' said Simon, unable to think of any device to prolong the interview further. 'I'm obliged to you both.'

He turned as he gained the street, to wave. The man in the old fawn cardigan stood in the doorway, ingratiatingly smiling. He gave a stiff wave, as if it was a habit he'd never got accustomed to. In the shadow of the hall loomed the bulky figure of the old woman. Then the door was shut firmly.

Walking down the street, Simon felt grubby, and in some odd way diminished. These, surely were mean, shabby people—depressing if he put them in his mind beside the generosity and openness of Dot and Tom Cutheridge, of his father and mother. Was this man, of whom he had no memory, his father? Biologically, possibly, but in no other sense. And yet, oddly, Simon felt go through him a spurt of excitement; he experienced the zest of anticipation, a feeling that he had just accomplished the first stage of a great and difficult project. It was almost, he decided, like the thrill of a chase.

Ten days later he received a letter to say that the room was his. He paid rent for nearly six weeks before he actually moved down. He had a feeling that the Simmeters were rubbing their hands at having landed a right greenhorn.

'It might suit me very well,' said Simon in Leeds, packing up those exercise books of memories and impressions he had started eight years before and looked forward now to adding to, 'to be thought a greenhorn.'

CHAPTER 6

When Simon Cutheridge travelled down to London in the third week of June, 1964, he had gone beyond asking himself whether what he was doing was a sensible thing, or one that was likely to make him happier. It had become something there to be done—something to be undertaken stage by stage, like a programme of research. He had drawn a line under his period in Leeds with some relief: he had given away some of his possessions, stored others with friends. He was, now, the clothes he stood up in and the suitcases he carried. He knew that many children adopted at birth developed a niggling itch to ferret out the identities of their real mothers and fathers. How much more natural in him, he thought, who had a history before Yeasdon and the Cutheridges, to wish to blow the dust off that page of his life. He was Simon Cutheridge. But he was also, he felt sure, Simon Simmeter. Or some other Christian name—perhaps some other surname too—but at any rate part of the Simmeter family. For better or worse.

He took the Underground from King's Cross to the Angel, because he was not a young man who had yet got into the taxi habit. He was a healthy man, and it was not the suitcases he was lugging that made his heart beat so dramatically as he emerged from the poky entrance to the Angel. He put them down for a minute to steady himself, wiping his forehead. Then he took them up and began walking.

Miswell Terrace was only five minutes from the station. It was just before three when he rang the doorbell at No. 25, but it was not the old woman's steps he heard along the passage. When Leonard Simmeter opened the door he had on the same old fawn cardigan, buttoned over the waist, and he rubbed his hands in the same convulsive way. But this time he wore a prepared smile, and he seemed to have lost some of the unaccountable nervousness of their first meeting.

'Ah . . . get here all right? Have a good journey down?'

Simon uttered conventionalities to answer conventionalities as he was ushered into the depressing hall. Nothing had changed. An old mac and some women's coats were hung on hooks. A little table held an ancient china fruit bowl, with no fruit in it. The door to the Simmeters' living quarters had been meticulously shut.

'Yes,' said Simmeter, with that uneasy, almost shifty chattiness that showed it did not come naturally, 'I believe it's not a bad service to the North these days. Not that I've ever taken it. Been on the railways all my life, and never been north of Watford. You know us Londoners—we think we've got everything here.' He came to a stop like a deflated balloon. 'Well, I expect you'll be wanting to go up.'

He led the way up the narrow staircase, not offering to help with the suitcases. Simon blundered up after him. Lights were switched on, briefly and grudgingly.

'That's the bathroom and toilet,' said Simmeter, opening a door and briefly illuminating a room on the first floor. 'You share that with Miss Cosgrove on a 'first come' basis. There's a meter there—that prevents arguments, doesn't it? . . . Right, here we are.'

They had reached the top of the house. Simmeter put the key in the door, swung it open, and they walked into the dingy little room. All traces of the previous occupant had been carefully removed, so the room presented itself to Simon in all its dismal basicness.

'I think you'll be very cosy here,' said Leonard Simmeter, apparently quite sincerely, seemingly unconscious that rooms could be, should be, otherwise.

'I'm sure I shall,' said Simon heartily.

'How would you like to pay the rent, then?'

Simon had thought about that. He suspected that Simmeter, knowing he had a respectable and well-paid job, would like him to pay by cheque once a month. It looked better. But he needed to take all the meagre opportunities that offered of contact with the family.

'I'll pay weekly,' he said, drawing out his wallet. 'I can pay you for the first week now.'

'That's very nice,' said Simmeter, kneading his palms. It was the stimulus of money, Simon decided, that most often sent him into that routine. The notes were tucked away lovingly in a warm and greasy little notecase. 'It's nice to do business with a real gentleman. And are they hard to find these days! Mr Blore was not what *I'd* call reliable—but then, I'm old-fashioned. Standards aren't what they were, I know that. Now, here's the key to the room, and here are the keys to the front door. Hope you settle in all right.'

And before Simon had a chance to think up further conversational gambits to detain him, Len Simmeter was off down the stairs, leaving Simon to unpack his possessions and gaze at the muddy green wallpaper, peeling at the corners, at the depressing armchair with the shape of the springs visible through the seat, at the sofa-bed which seemed unlikely to be satisfactory in either of its functions. It was an odd sort of homecoming.

Over the next few days Simon's personality and preoccupations seemed to develop along two diverging lines. He had a daytime self at the Zoo, where the plunge into his new job was hectic and stimulating, his colleagues welcoming and forthcoming. It was a job that absorbed him entirely, but only while he was doing it. He found himself fending off or postponing offers of hospitality, suggestions of drinks after work.

Because there was, slumbering uneasily, that early morning and evening self. This self sat in the damp and constricting little room, waiting and watching for wisps of information, possibilities of contact, with the Simmeter family two floors below. The evenings were spent reading, making coffee, having a whisky—and listening, always listening; treasuring up a scrap of a sentence, identifying footsteps, classifying ingrained habits and wondering how to make use of them. Up there at the top of the house, cut off by doors and staircases and the deep-rooted secrecy of the people themselves, he felt like a far from omniscient God, reduced to judging his creations by overheard whispers, by occasional glimpses, by fragments of behaviour that penetrated by freaks of the atmosphere to his heavenly fastness.

There were more Simmeters than he had so far met, that he concluded early on. They slept on the first floor, and all three bedrooms there were occupied. Each night, through the crack of his door that he left slightly ajar, he heard three separate sets of footsteps mount the first flight of stairs: first the old woman—slow and heavy, but without help; then, as a rule, Len—fussily closing the door to the ground-floor rooms, checking the front door, and turning off the lights as quickly as possible; then, he was fairly sure, a woman's—less careful with the door, leaving lights on while she went to the bathroom, once leaving them on after she had gone to bed, so that he heard Len come out and switch them off, muttering bitterly. These last two sets of footsteps sometimes came in a different order, but they never came together.

The view from his poky garret window was unsatisfactory. By no kind of bodily contortion could he see the tiny front garden, like a folded pocket handkerchief, or the iron gate. But he could see the pavement in front of the house, and on three successive mornings he saw a woman with faded fair hair who seemed to have just turned—to have come out of the gate, and then turned in the direction of the tube station. And it was not Miss Cosgrove, from the room opposite his.

He had said 'Good Morning' and 'Good Evening' to Miss Cosgrove two or three times by the end of the first week. He had not wanted to rush into engaging her in conversation. He felt instinctively that the secrecy of the Simmeter family was part of a larger secrecy or wariness that was a birthright of Londoners—an obsessive guarding of their privacy, a blank front to the world's curiosity. The unfriendliness of Londoners had been part of the received wisdom of Yeasdon, in spite of the manifest openness and forthrightness of most of the kids who had landed on them during the war. Their parents, Yeasdon knew, would be different: you could have the same neighbour in London for thirty years and not swap more than the occasional good-morning with him. Thus, making no distinction between Wimbledon or West Ham, Kensington or Kentish Town, the Yeasdoners confidently pronounced on the mores of the capital, on the strength of their day trips to Oxford Street and a nice play.

So Simon was a little nervous one evening, when he had been in Miswell Terrace a matter of ten days, when out of the blue he invited Miss Cosgrove in. He was on his way down to fill his kettle from the bathroom tap and when he met Miss Cosgrove coming up the invitation in for coffee seemed to present itself naturally.

'Well, that's kind of you. Thank you very much,' she said, after a moment's hesitation, and clearly surprised. She and Mr Blore, it seemed, had not fraternized. When she came in a few minutes later the kettle was beginning to sing. She looked around the room—at the Constable and Canaletto prints, at the Beatles poster and the embroidered bedspread that his mother had sent him, and said:

'Well, you've done what you could. I don't think anyone could make this room really pleasant.'

'I suspect you're right. It's only temporary. I don't want to commit myself to a flat till I know London better.'

'That's probably wise. I've never gone in for a flat myself because there are other things I prefer to spend my money on, but sometimes I think there are areas I'd prefer to live in. Where do you work?'

'I'm on the scientific staff at the London Zoo.'

That set Miss Cosgrove going, and got the conversation off to a good start. Miss Cosgrove was not an imaginative soul, and the inherent sadness of the Zoo had never struck her: the London Zoo was her idea of a good day out, she said. She'd taken her mother, five years ago, it must be now, the last time the old lady had managed a day in London. And she'd been back two or three times since. You could spend a whole day there, and still there'd be lots of things left that you wished you'd seen.

Miss Cosgrove was in her early forties: desperately unstylish, but sensible and straightforward. She had a mother in Sussex somewhere, but she had adapted to London, and dreaded the possibility that some day she might have to go back and look after her mother. She managed a law stationer's off Holborn, and loved living near the opera. So cheap! she said. In fact, she seemed to be one of those Londoners who relished everything it had to offer. Simon found himself volunteering to show her round the Zoo, when he had got to know it better himself.

'Oh, that *is* kind of you. I would enjoy that, because you learn so much more when you're with someone who really knows. I'm a demon for learning things. I suppose it's some sort of puritan conscience coming out in a funny way. I like to get something *out* of what I do.'

'Yes,' said Simon. 'I suppose I'm the same.'

'After all, when you've got all those theatres and galleries and museums within easy reach, you ought to make use of them, oughtn't you? And evening classes. That's where I've been tonight—one on Italian civilization, because I'm off to Florence in September. I always seem to be going somewhere or studying something. I'd rather spend my money on that than on a bigger flat.'

'You've been here a long time?'

'Longer than I care to think. Seventeen years or so. Not that there haven't been efforts to get me out.'

'Really? Why would Mr Simmeter do that?'

'Because I rented the room unfurnished, so the rent is controlled: they can't put it up, not by more than a pittance. If I got out they could try various fiddles—doing bogus improvements, and then applying to put it up. It was Mother that tried first. A very forceful lady she used to be. Definitely failing by now, of course. Then the son tried—he's the same type, but he hasn't got the same confidence.'

'Do you know them well?'

'Just to hand the rent to—and argue with, if they try anything on.'

'You don't visit down there?'

'Good Lord, no. Why would I do that? I don't think the Simmeters have much to offer anybody.'

She seemed to find the suggestion odd, so Simon hastened to justify his curiosity.

'It's just that where I come from, in the West Country, it would seem a bit funny—living on top of a family all these years and hardly knowing them.'

'It's perfectly normal here. Funny—I'd have said you came from the North.'

Simon bent to get the kettle, to hide a blush.

'I've lived in Leeds for five years. You pick up the accent quickly. I expect I'll talk London soon.'

'There's no London accent, only different accents from different parts,' said Miss Cosgrove, in her didactic but rather pleasant way. 'Remember Professor Higgins in *Pygmalion*? Round here there's a tremendous conglomeration of accents—there's so much of a floating population. There is a basic Islington accent, but it's a long time before you pick it out. The Simmeters, now: they're not local.'

'Are they not?' asked Simon, with that quick blush of embarrassment again. Miss Cosgrove's openness and directness made him conscious of his own deviousness.

'No—West London somewhere. I couldn't pin it down. I did a course on London dialects once, but I've forgotten most of it. Now Connie—she's got an overlay of something else. She's worked somewhere, or tried to lose her accent, or something.'

'Connie?'

'She's the sister; you may not have met her yet. More

presentable than the others, and can affect the genteel when she feels like it. Unmarried, like me. We did get together and have a bit of a chat once—ten or twelve years ago, it must be—but we didn't really click. You don't click, with the Simmeters.'

'Is Len unmarried too?'

'Well, he is now. I think he has been married—yes, I remember: we were talking once about how unfair the tax system is to the single person—that's Len Simmeter's type of conversation, though it's perfectly true as well—and he described himself as a widower. Though when people say that, they're just as often divorced, and don't want to admit it for some reason. It wouldn't be surprising if he were, and I'd never blame the wife: he's not someone most women would fancy.'

Miss Cosgrove stood up.

'Aren't we gossiping? Well, that was nice. I'd better get across the way before I start slandering anyone else. I've got tickets for *Othello* tomorrow night, and I really ought to get in a bit of homework.'

Miss Cosgrove, Simon felt, had earned her conducted tour of the Zoo. The next day, when he saw a faded blonde head turn in the street below the house, he said to himself: 'There's Connie.'

He had kicked himself after Miss Cosgrove left for not asking precisely what Leonard Simmeter did on the railways. It wasn't the sort of thing you could bring up casually when you met on the stairs. But, as it happened, he found out unexpectedly two days later.

He was leaving the house, as usual, at about five to nine, and from the front door of No. 23 a young girl came out, and they banged doors together. Twenty, in a red, short skirt, bright as new paint, and glorying in being young in the era of the young. She was the sort of girl you had to smile at, and the smile she gave Simon back was brilliant, open, and frankly interested.

'Hello,' she said chirpily, with a faint trace of cockney accent, and reminding Simon of a cock-a-hoop London sparrow. 'Moved next door, have you?'

'That's right. About a fortnight ago.

'Room all right?'

'Not too bad,' said Simon, as they began walking along Miswell Terrace together. 'A bit dismal.'

'I know. They mostly are in this area. That's why they're cheap, isn't it? I wouldn't have expected that you'd get anything very cheery with that creepy lot.'

'The Simmeters? Do you know them?'

'No. Just seen them coming in and out now and again. They look a bit—you know—yukky.'

'Oh, they're all right. I haven't seen much of them.'

'I don't suppose you will. My landlady says they keep themselves to themselves. Mind you, there was all that trouble last year, and that brought him out a bit.'

'Trouble?'

'At the tube, where he works. I wasn't here then, but my landlady told me. He's got a temper, has your Mr Simmeter. And he's sort of Deputy Station Master, or whatever the pecking order is, down the road, at the Angel. Anyway, he got on his high horse, started giving someone a real dressing-down—one of the guards or something—and it was downright abuse, and there was practically a strike. There was a stoppage, and it went to arbitration, and he was censured—you know the kind of thing. It got in all the local papers, because of the inconvenience the stoppage caused. He was interviewed—imagine! My landlady said she learned more about the Simmeters that week than she'd learnt in the whole twenty years they'd lived next door.'

'So she doesn't know them well?'

'Hardly at all. Well—this is me. 'Bye for now.'

And giving him a smile that said she wouldn't mind talking to him again if he was interested, she turned into a little hairdresser's. Simon continued on to the tube.

That tube station, the Angel, now had an added interest for him, but it was not one it was easy to satisfy. It was hardly a place where one could stand around and gawp—one passed through it on the way to the platforms. There was a dim little hall, with ticket office and ticket machines, with a couple of lifts to your left. There were no signs of offices, and you were not very likely to see a Deputy Station Master on the platforms. The most one could do was go through it more slowly than before, fumble for change by the machines, display interest in a poster. On the way back the possibilities were even more limited. For several days Simon was on the alert without ever catching a glimpse of Len Simmeter. His irregular hours were now explained: he worked on some kind of shift, so there was no calculating times when he might leave in the mornings or come home at nights. Simon was beginning to think that the best thing would be to start leaving for work at the same time as Connie, the sister, when, five days after his chat with his neighbour, he got out of the lift in the evening and saw the back of Len's head through the grimy glass of the ticket office. He had his overcoat on, and seemed to be giving instructions to the man on duty. Simon dawdled outside, buying a chocolate bar at the kiosk, and as he counted out the money Len Simmeter came out of the station and turned towards home.

'Signing off for the day?' said Simon, coming up behind him in the sunny evening street. Leonard Simmeter jumped, as perhaps it was in his nature to do.

'Ah—Good evening, Mr Cutheridge! Lovely evening, eh? Really warm and nice. Yes, I've just knocked off. So you've found me out at my place of work?'

'That's right. I saw you coming out from behind the scenes. Nice quiet little station, is it?'

'Not bad. Not too bad. I'm used to it now—worked here for years. Used to be in a much busier set-up, but you don't want that as you start getting older. No, this suits me fine. And what about yourself? Settled in nicely at the Zoo?'

'Yes, I think so. I'm enjoying it, at any rate.'

'That's good. That's very satisfactory. Because it's what I call a good job—satisfying, responsible, with a bit of class. And o' course, being on the scientific side you'd be one of the bigwigs, wouldn't you?'

He was looking at Simon in an ingratiating way, trying to flatter his youthful ego, but not having the subtlety to do it successfully. Simon had rarely seen eyes that spoke more definitely of calculation.

'Not one of the bigwigs by a long chalk, I'm afraid.'

'You shouldn't sell yourself down,' urged Len, and added with an uneasy laugh: 'You're certainly not one of the shit-shovellers.'

'No—you could say I'm betwixt and between.'

'Like there'd be some sort of Board over you, running the place?'

'That's right. They keep out of the limelight, but that's what happens. They're Establishment men: retired politicians, eminent scientists, civil servants. And business men—rich as Jews, mostly, and they're very useful because they advise about marketing, investment, promoting the place in one way or another. It's the Board who are God Almighties at the Zoo. We on the scientific staff cut a pretty poor figure.'

'Ah well—you do get some pretty funny people running things these days.' Len shot Simon a nervous glance, then clutched the old mac he was carrying over his arm in spite of the warmth of the sun. 'Still—I can see you're one young man who's going to the top. That's for sure. I can tell.'

Simon laughed.

'I don't know that I'm all that interested in getting to the top. So long as I've got a job I like, I'm quite happy.'

'You're too modest. But you're quite right. That is the main thing in life. And a nice place to live, where you can be nice and cosy.' They turned in at the gate. 'You are nice and cosy up there, I hope?'

'Fine, just fine. I'll start getting to know the neighbourhood soon, when I've less to do at the job. I think I'll start going to the opera, when the season starts. And get to know the pubs . . . '

'That's right. That's right.'

Leonard Simmeter stood uneasily in the hall, as if the forms of social intercourse sat uneasily on him, and he could not find the acceptable way to say goodnight. He seemed half to want to dive into the Simmeter fastness, half to want to stay and be friendly.

'Perhaps,' said Simon, jumping in earlier than he had intended, 'perhaps we could go out for a drink together some night?'

'Perhaps we might,' said Len Simmeter, his hand on the door into his living quarters. '*She* wouldn't approve. And I'm not a drinking man normally. But perhaps we might.'

He turned back towards Simon and fixed him with a cracked, nervous, ingratiating smile.

'I've taken quite a shine to you, young man.'

CHAPTER 7

When Simon Cutheridge did at length gain admittance to the Simmeters' domestic fortress, it was not through the medium of Len. There was no follow-up to those parting words, in spite of their rather off-putting friendliness. The routines of the ground floor followed their unchanging pattern: each night three pairs of footsteps were heard as the family put themselves to bed; and in the daytime when Simon was home, fragments of the beginnings or ends of conversations floated up the stairs, before the door to the living quarters was closed. These fragments were almost always unrevealing: 'No, I won't forget to buy potatoes' was one; 'I'm early tonight, Mother' was another. True he did once hear a woman's voice—Connie's?—say: 'Well, he's done it once before, hasn't he?' and something spiteful in the voice, and the banged door that followed, made Simon note it down in that exercise book that he had started years before in Yeasdon. But when he took up the book and looked through all the entries he had made since he arrived in

Miswell Terrace, he felt that no degree of optimism could suggest that they were likely to be of use. He had the feeling that if the Simmeters had anything of importance to say, anything that might be a clue to the Simmeter mentality, they would make sure they went in and closed the connecting door before they said it.

Except, perhaps, for the sister—for Connie. About a week after his talk with Len he heard her again. This time the voice was raised, and again it was followed by a banged door. Connie seemed to make a speciality of exit lines. What she said was: 'That's how you've always been, Len, and I was a fool to think you might change now.' The tone was more that of a self-satisfied jeer than of bitterness, and it was clearly the concluding remark in a family row. The words in themselves told him next to nothing, but they persuaded him that Connie might be worth cultivating. There must, surely, be a Simmeter capable of unbuttoning.

It was ten days after his talk with Len that Simon, early back from work, rang the Simmeters' bell as he let himself into 25, Miswell Terrace, and stood in the little hall fumbling for his wallet to pay the week's rent. From the back of the house could be heard the inevitable slow shuffle as old Mrs Simmeter came towards the connecting door and opened it.

'Ah. You'll be wanting to pay your rent. I thought it might be that, so I brought the book.'

The old woman shut the door, and heaved herself up the two steps into the hall. Then she sat down on a spindly little chair by the hall table, laboriously placed a piece of carbon paper between the leaves of the receipt book, accepted Simon's proffered four pound notes and a ten shilling one, and began writing slowly. Her fat breasts heaved as she took wheezy, constricted breaths—breaths that ended in a high whistle, like a kettle about to boil.

'Lovely afternoon again,' said Simon.

'Is it? Down there you don't notice the weather. I don't get out much these days.'

'That's a pity, on a fine day like this.'

'I dunno. Nowhere to go in Islington that I haven't been more than enough times. I can just about get to the shops, if Len's late and can't go.'

'He's a good son to you.'

'He lives here. He has to do his bit.'

'And you've got your daughter.'

'Hmmm. *She* lives here, but it's no good relying on *her* for much. Well, there you are.' She handed him the receipt— 'Received from S. Cutheridge the sum of £4.10.0. Signed Flora Simmeter'—and began putting the worn scrap of carbon under the next receipt. Then she stood up.

'Well, good afternoon to you.'

It was extraordinarily difficult to engage the Simmeters in conversation. Even the minimal courtesies of life were distributed as if they were hard dog biscuits. The old woman began to shuffle back to her lair, apparently anxious once more to put that peeling varnished door between herself and the world. Simon was starting unhappily up the stairs when he was arrested by a cry.

'Oh! Oh my God!'

Mrs Simmeter was clutching at the little rail on the wall, and her face was twisted with pain. Clearly her ankle had gone from under her as she eased herself down the two steps towards the connecting door.

'Here,' said Simon, his heart leaping with anticipation as he ran down to her. 'Look, rest on me. Rest your weight on my shoulder. That's right. Take the bad foot off the ground.'

'I'll be all right in a minute. Don't tell Len you had to help me. It's my wonky ankle—never can trust it. But it's never been as bad as this before.'

Without asking permission Simon leaned adroitly forward and threw open the door to the Simmeters' quarters.

'Now—you've got to sit down and put the foot up. If you can try to put most of your weight on the good foot, I'll take the weight on the other side.'

Together they went through the door and into the murky passage. It was dimly lit like the hall, and papered in the same dispiriting pattern. On the left was a door, shut, that must lead to the dining room—unused, Simon guessed, having glimpsed it through the window from the street. Ahead, at the end of the passage, was a large kitchen, and off to the right was another door. The old woman gestured in its direction.

'In there. The end door. I can sit on the sofa.'

As the two made their slow and painful progress towards the door, and through it, and across the room to the sofa, Simon was thinking: I must be sensible. Keep a grip on myself. No swooning, like that first time in Farrow Street. No fits of the megrims if I recognize anything. It's what I expect to do anyway. And if I go over faint, there'll be two of us on the floor.

The thought of that made a chuckle go through his body. The old woman felt it, and threw him a sour look, as if she distrusted his kindness and thought he was laughing at her. Simon concentrated anew on his task, looking straight ahead.

The room was very much what he might have expected. The Simmeter family seemed to have a bias towards browns and muddy greens. The wallpaper had once been a fawn embossed one, but age had darkened it. The sofa towards which he was inching the old lady was heavy and hideous, and it was covered with a thick, prickly material in dark greens and purples that had shaded, with time, towards black. There were two bulky matching armchairs. They sent no shock of recognition to Simon's brain. He eased Mrs Simmeter down on to one end of the sofa.

'There,' he said, in the tones of his stepfather. 'Easy does it.'

'Oh. Oh dear. Ah—that's better.'

'Now you've just got to rest it.'

'Don't tell Len, will you?' She added with the fierceness of declining powers: 'He *seizes* on things like this!'

'I should think Len will see when he comes in. I don't think you'll be using this leg again today. Anyway,

I think you should put it up.'

She seemed not to want him to touch her, and she herself painfully raised the hurt foot up on to the sofa.

'I'm much obliged to you,' she said—grudgingly, as if thanks were to be distributed sparingly, like ha'pence on Guy Fawkes Night. 'I'll be all right now. Sorry to have inconvenienced you.'

'No inconvenience at all. It looks very swollen. Do you have anything you put on it?'

'No. It'll go down of its own accord.'

'Can I get you anything? Can I make you a cup of tea, perhaps?'

'No, there's no call. Perhaps a glass of water.'

As they talked, Simon had been looking round the room. The only decorations on the wall were two old engravings, mottled brown with age. The carpet was threadbare, and added no light or colour to the room. All the furniture was dark, massive, disfigured by bulbous—

That was it. The shock of recognition. It came as he was looking at the legs of the sideboard. It was a long, solid construction, formed in the days when furniture was furniture, and built all too inevitably to last. It stood on four hideous and dropsical legs—each one a great bulbous sphere, with smaller spheres above and beneath, and echoed by similar protuberances poking out of the doors like goitres. But it was the legs that flashed to Simon's mind a vision—of himself, sitting on the floor, very small, dwarfed by this great palace of a sideboard, running his hand over this polished globe and turning it in his mind's eye into a pumpkin—the pumpkin that in one of his books turned into a carriage in which the Prince and Princess rode away, but which in his fantasy became a pumpkin airliner that took him to the moon.

'Oh yes. Of course. A glass of water,' he said.

The kitchen was cream-painted, with a linoleum floor. Lighter and pleasanter than the sitting-room, it was yet featureless, with no trace of a joy in food—with no trace of food at all, since everything had been put neatly back in its place behind cupboard doors. Simon pulled open one or two of the doors, found a glass, and filled it from the tap. As he returned with it to the shadowy sitting-room, his eyes darted round for objects of interest, and then fixed themselves on three family photographs. Two were on the sideboard, one on a little occasional table behind the sofa. As he passed the sideboard he ignored the picture of a young man in an RAF cap and tunic—a young man who bore no resemblance to Len—and took up instead a wedding photograph in a tarnished frame.

'I love family photographs,' he said.

His tone sounded unconvincing even to himself, but once the old woman had shot him a sharp, contemptuous glance, she went back to rubbing her ankle.

'So your son's been married, has he?'

The picture was brown with age and not very clear. It showed a much younger Len Simmeter, in lounge suit with wide lapels and baggy trousers, standing in the doorway of a red brick, neo-Gothic church. On his arm was a mildly pretty woman whose manner was somehow uncertain, as if she hardly knew how to cope with this big day in her life, as if she hardly knew how she came to be marrying at all. The uncertainty of manner contrasted oddly with her clothes, since she was wearing what would then have been called a costume, and a smart one, and on her head was a sideways-tilted hat with a feather that curled round her ear. It was as if she had bought clothes that clashed entirely with her personality and fate. The clothes were, somehow, someone else's, while the manner was her own.

'Oh yes, Len was married. They didn't have a white wedding. It's a waste, I said to them, when you've no use for the dress afterwards. You dye it and it still looks like a wedding dress. Then she spent all that money on that flashy costume.'

She seemed to remember the clothes, but to have forgotten the people.

'And she's—not still alive?'

'Oh no. Dead. She died in the war. We're an unlucky family. Had more than our fair share, I can tell you.'

She doled out these little driblets of information and complaint with the same grudgingness that seemed to characterize all her actions and attitudes. Simon brought over the glass of water, put it in her hand, and then stationed himself behind the sofa. Here he could see the other photograph, and, unwatched, could print it on his mind. While the fat old woman drank, resting the glass on her heavy breasts, he quietly squatted on his haunches and looked close.

It was the same woman as in the wedding photograph. Len Simmeter's wife. My mother, thought Simon? A little older now, but still looking somehow as if she were adrift in the world. Only in the eyes, which were beautiful, was there any suggestion that somewhere there might be reserves of purpose. By her side, clutching her skirts, was a small boy of perhaps two, looking at the camera with that posed sweetness that a studio portraitist at that time probably insisted upon.

Me, thought Simon to himself. That must be me.

He looked into the boy's eyes, hoping for a moment of recognition, an uprush of memories. None came. Me—but *another* me, thought Simon sadly.

He wanted desperately to ask more questions. After a struggle he restrained himself. One or two questions might be regarded as natural, as a display of merely polite interest. To ask more would seem nosey, especially to the Simmeters. To show a close interest in them as a family might be to shut that door against him for ever. Simon came from behind the sofa, and took the glass out of the old lady's hand.

'Now, you're sure there's nothing more I can do?'

'No. No, there's nothing more. Len'll be home soon. I suppose I'll have to tell him.' And as Simon made reluctantly for the door, she brought out that grudging 'Thanks.' Squeezing the last toothpaste from the tube would seem easier.

It was later that same evening that Simon heard well-known footsteps up the stairs, and then a tap on his door. Simon had been entering things in his notebooks, and in fact had started a sketchbook in which he had made versions of the two photographs he had looked at closely, to fix them in his memory. He had no great skill with the pencil, but after three or four attempts he thought he had caught something of the woman's face in both pictures, given some idea of the clothes, the church, caught the feeling of the picture of the mother and son. Then he had begun to jot down various possible lines of inquiry, paths into the great areas of grey matter that still remained: the registers of the Paddington churches; the local newspapers; more people who might remember the Simmeters in Farrow Street, or old colleagues of Len's at Paddington Station.

When he heard the footsteps begin the ascent to the second floor, he turned over the pages of his notebook to a blank one.

'Oh, er, Mr Cutheridge, sorry to interrupt—'

Len Simmeter's head came round the door.

'No—not at all. I'm not doing anything important.'

'I know you intellectuals. Never want the flow of thought broken in on. And quite right too. No, I just wanted to thank you for what you did for Mother this afternoon.'

'It was nothing. The least I could do.'

'It was most kind and much appreciated. Poor old Ma—she's failing a bit now. Doesn't like it known—as perhaps you noticed?'

'Yes, I did.'

'She's been a fine woman all her life. Firm. Determined. The backbone of the family, in good times and bad. Hates her own weakness, she does. It's terrible for us to watch her cracking up like this.'

But there was a glint in Simmeter's eye, and he had resumed that nervous rubbing of his palms. He gave Simon the impression that the crack-up was not entirely unwelcome.

'She seemed to have all her faculties,' said Simon. 'There didn't seem to be any mental crack-up.'

'She hasn't got the concentration she once had. The purpose. She was always the one to take the decisions. Now she finds she's having to hand over to—someone else.' He took a step into the room. 'Well, you have got it nice in here, young feller. That's Venice, isn't it? Tell by the gondolas. Never got beyond Rome, myself. Fine city. Wonderful city.'

'Were you there in the war?'

'Before. Long before. Well, it *is* very tasteful and homely in here now. Not like when the other one was here.'

'Mr Blore?'

'Put up political posters, can you imagine? Political posters in your own bedroom. I've never heard the like. He'll be well punished if his lot gain power, that's one consolation. But you've got it very nice. You've got discrimination, that's what you've got!'

The flattery was too laughable to follow up. Simon said:

'Your mother's all right now?'

'She's fine. I made her some nice soup, and she got that down. Connie—that's my sister—she's home now, and she'll put her to bed. I've told her she's got to put her to bed. Oh yes, Mother will be back on her feet in a couple of days—thanks to you, young man.'

'Not at all. We must have that drink some time.'

'That's right. We must.' He rubbed his hands again, as if making up his mind to it took a great deal of effort. 'Tomorrow's Saturday, and that's always a bit rowdy. I don't like a rowdy crowd myself—no more do you, I'm sure. Lot of rough types around here: it's a mixed area, and no mistake. Mother would worry if I went out to a pub on Saturday, and I want to spare her poor old mind any worry. Likewise Sunday is against her principles. Well—let's say Monday.'

'Monday. That would be fine.'

'Nice quiet time of the week. We can have a nice chat without being disturbed. I'm not one for sing-songs and that sort of thing, but I do like a good chat.' He smiled once more that twisted, hesitant, unaccustomed smile. 'I think you and I see eye to eye over a lot of things, young feller. I'm looking forward to having a nice chat with you.'

That was my father, said Simon to himself as the footsteps receded down the stairs. That night he was surprised to wake up in the long watches and find he had been crying.

CHAPTER 8

The Colonel Monk was a terrible pub. As a place for a boys' night out together it was convenient, but it certainly wasn't desirable. It was just round the corner from the Simmeters, in Marbury Street, and Simon had suggested they go somewhere quiet. The Colonel Monk was quiet because it was not very nice. True, it was untouched by the modernizer's hand, but then it seemed pretty well untouched by the cleaner's as well. The acres of dark varnish presented a sticky as well as a smoky aspect, and many of the advertisers' placards around the walls and over the bar were for types of cigarettes no longer on the market, brands of spirits no longer distilled. The landlord was surly, and pulled a vile pint, and the clientele stared at their glasses, dropped ash into their laps, and edged reluctantly aside to let them order at the bar.

'Well, this is cosy,' said Len. 'Very cosy indeed.'

Len used the words 'nice' and 'cosy' very frequently, Simon had noticed, and seemed to have redefined them in his own image. As he put the money down on the bar for two cloudy pints of bitter, Len looked around him.

'Teddy drops in here now and again. When he's home on a visit. He's more fond of his beer than I am, is Teddy.'

'Teddy?'

'My younger brother. Very sociable type, Teddy.'

Which no doubt accounted for the fact that on his occasional visits to his family he felt the need to go out to a pub. Simon took up his glass, and they made for a chilly little corner. On the small round table there, rings from the morning's drinking could be seen, and a filter stub nestled coyly in the ashtray. Len took the cushioned seat by the wall, and Simon took the chair opposite.

'It's quiet here too,' continued Len. 'None of the local riff-raff and coloureds. They go up the road, to the Jolly Beagle. When you've got a job like mine you get enough brawling and shouting, without getting it when you go out for the evening as well.'

'It's bad on the Underground, is it?'

'Diabolical. Bloody appalling. Not to mention the petty crime as well. There's no backbone in the country any longer, but you might hope that people still had an ounce of honesty—but no, not on your life. It's not as bad as New York, but it's getting that way, I can tell you. You were lucky, young feller, that you grew up in the country.'

'I suppose I was.'

'Not that it was like this then. It's all happened in the last ten or fifteen years. And we all know who's to blame! Where was it you said you grew up, young Simon?'

Simon swallowed, kept his eyes on Len's face, and said: 'Yeasdon.'

There was not the slightest flicker of a reaction. Not a blink, not a twitching nerve.

'And where would that be? Up north somewhere?'

'No, Gloucestershire. Not far from Bristol.'

'Ah yes. Can't say I know those parts very well. Now Surrey and Sussex I know, because we used to go there for holidays—day trips too, sometimes, because I got free travel on the rail. That was before the war—and after, once or twice. Now and then I used to go further afield—abroad, you know. But that was a big adventure then. Not like now, when all the hoi-polloi go on these package tours. Still, I really ought to be ashamed I don't know my own country better. So you grew up in Yeasdon, did you? And what does your father do?'

'He was a stockman on one of the local estates. He had an accident, and he really only jobs around the place now.'

'Well, well: sort of farm labourer, eh? You have gone far and no mistake, young feller. I admire you for it. Too little of that sort of initiative around these days.'

'I don't know about initiative. I just did reasonably well at school, and the rest seemed to follow.'

'But there you are, you see: a good brain, and a bit of encouragement in the home—that's what does it. Now I never had encouragement in the home. Not to speak ill of Mother, but she always wanted us out, earning. Naturally, since she was on her own. Dad died soon after Teddy was born, so Mother has always been head of the family. Until now—now she's failing, like you've seen. Naturally Mother wanted money coming in. I never resented it, but I think Connie did. Could have made a nice little career for herself, if she'd had the education. A real career, I mean—like yours is shaping up to be.' He looked at him intently over his beer glass. 'Already you're mixing with the nobs.'

'Mostly with giraffes and seals, actually.'

'Oh no—like you said, there's all those big boys on the Board. What did you call them? Establishment men. Not to mention the fat boys with the long purses and the crooked noses.'

Simon flinched inwardly at the crudity of his companion. At the same time he was conscious of being watched. Not looked at, but watched.

'Oh, they're people quite apart, really,' he said, studiedly neutral. 'They come in once a month, have a day-long meeting and a slap-up lunch, and then we hear what's been decided. We hardly ever get to meet them.'

'Ah,' said Len, his eyes still on Simon. 'It's a funny old world, isn't it? Lots of funny people in control, eh?'

Simon shifted uneasily in his chair. The conversation was

taking a direction he had hardly envisaged, and one he hardly knew how to cope with politely. Far from being cosy or intimate, the atmosphere seemed to have become fraught with an inexplicable tension. He felt, oddly, as if *he* were being sounded out by *Len*—quite the reverse of what he had intended.

'At the moment I'm not too much worried about who's in control, just in getting on top of my job,' he said. And then, trying to take over the rudder of the conversation, he added: 'If I have got anywhere, I put it down to my family. Encouragement in the home counts for an awful lot, as you say. And then having a united family—as your own is . . . '

'Yes. Quite.' Len's body seemed to lose its tension, as if he were backing away from a perilous leap. 'You could say Mother kept us together. Teddy fled the nest, in a manner of speaking, first with the war, then getting married not long after. But otherwise we've all mostly muddled along together.'

'Even when you got married, in your case, I believe?'

'That's right. Oh—you saw the pictures, did you? The Ma sets great store by them pictures. Very fond memories she has—we both have, of course. Yes, when I got hitched I brought her back to live with Mother. Well—it was the only sensible thing to do, granted the size of the house, and that.'

'The house you live in now?'

'No—over Paddington way. I used to work in the ticket office of the station—that was before nationalization, of course. The GWR Station it was then. The house in Paddington was a bit of a barn, and back in the 'thirties no one was buying places like that, so Mother would have been stuck. So naturally we moved in with her.'

'People say you should never have two women sharing a kitchen.'

Len, for some reason, leaned back in his seat and laughed uproariously, as if Simon had made a witticism.

'Depends on the ladies—eh, young feller? Well, we had

three in our house, at any rate three as soon as war broke out. I won't say there wasn't a spot of argy-bargy now and then, because there was. Connie's got a bit of a temper—not that *she* was often in the kitchen, oh no!—and Mother knows her own mind, or did then. But it was Mary who kept the peace. My Mary. She was a quiet soul, religious you might almost say, but she was a little wonder when it came to smoothing over unpleasantness. It was Mary who kept things on an even keel. I was proud of her, by golly I was!'

There was something deeply unconvincing about Len when he spoke forcefully, like a politician with a prepared brief.

'You must have been very happy,' said Simon.

'Oh, we were. Idyllically. I hope when you find yourself a nice young lady that you're half as happy as we were.'

'I hope so. I didn't do too well first time around.'

Len put his glass down on the table, pushed himself back on his seat, and looked at Simon with concern.

'Well, strike a light! Don't tell me you've been married.'

'I'm afraid so. It didn't work out.'

'Well, I'd never have thought it. How old are you? And divorced!'

'Separated. We will get divorced. I'm twenty-eight.'

'Dear me. And that's *not* old. You could knock me down with a feather. Here's me thinking of you as fresh out in the big wide world, and now it turns out you've been hitched, and not just hitched but separated and all. Well, I am sad. Like I would be if you was my own son. It's the way of the world these days, I suppose. It wasn't like that in my generation, I can tell you. For better or worse, that's what we believed. All I can say is: you try a bit harder next time, son.'

'Oh, I mean to,' said Simon, flinching at that casual use of the word 'son'.

'Take your time. Look about you.' Len was becoming more expansive, as if the role of counsellor to the young was one he relished. 'The fact is, you're a nice-looking,

well-set-up young fellow, in a good line of work. There's
plenty around would like to get their hands on you for that
reason alone. Keep a weather eye out. Take a bit of care.
You want to be a bit luckier next time.'

'That's what my mother says.'

'And she's dead right. You want to find a nice, quiet girl
who'll devote herself to you, body and soul; one who'll be a
help in your career.' He made it sound quite deadly. He
thinks I should marry someone who's only half alive,
thought Simon. 'Someone who'll work for you, unobtrusive
like, in the background. Bring up your kids in the right way,
the old-fashioned way. That's what you want. That's what
I call a happy marriage.'

'Like yours,' said Simon.

'That's right. Like mine. Because Mary was a self-effacing
soul, and the better for it. Not that she couldn't stand up
for herself if needs be. But there'd be no argument for the
sake of argument. Mary knew there was nothing to be gained
by that. Even when we married—don't get me wrong, young
feller, we were in love, oh my word yes—but there was also
her Pa, and my Ma, both strong churchgoers. Baptists, they
were—the Ma still is: can't get there often, but the Minister
calls. So Mother and Mr Spurling, they thought it would
be ideal if we two got married and set up home in Farrow
Street (that was where we lived). They thought it all out
between them. And Mary was influenced, naturally, because
her father was a very fine man—real head of the family, like
you had in the old days. So we got married, and you might
say that love, in the fullest sense of the word, came later.'

Len seemed somewhat confused as to when love had
come, and Simon was not convinced it had come at all. Len,
perhaps unused to being listened to so meekly, was now in
fine flow, more unbuttoned than Simon had dared to hope.
His long, angular body had relaxed from its usual spasmodic
tenseness, and the watchful testing of Simon had been
forgotten. He sat, relaxed and reminiscent, over his empty
glass. Simon nimbly fetched him another, and then said:

'And of course you had the little boy, didn't you, to bring you close together?'

'We did. Later on we had him. You saw that picture, did you? Had that taken in the war, when the raids started, thinking you never knew what might happen. How right I was! Now it's my only memento. Though that's not true: I've got my memories. And they're the best mementoes, aren't they?'

Len dabbed at his eyes, and Simon had to repress an involuntary retch of disgust.

'She looked as if she'd be a very good mother,' he said.

'Oh, she was. Second to none. It was what she lived for. I just can't describe how happy she was when she realized a little one was on the way. Over the moon she was—in her quiet way, of course. Not demonstrative, because Mother wasn't so happy about having a baby in the house. But Mary'd always been a real little mother to any stray kids around—a sort of auntie to lots of kids at church, taught Sunday School, and that. And when she had her own! Well, you should have seen her starting off my little David learning the alphabet when he was no age at all! She'd sit with him over a picture book with them great big letters, and she'd say them over with him, having him recognizing words. Tiny scrap of a lad, too! It was a picture, I tell you, to see them sitting together in the armchair, going through their kiddies' books. It's one of the last memories I have.'

'He must have been a . . . bright little boy.'

'Oh, he was. No question, he was. Couldn't hardly recognize him as my own.' Len gave a self-deprecating smile of the sort that really conceals an immense self-satisfaction. 'He picked up things that quick, you wouldn't believe. She used to bring him down sometimes to Paddington, when I was on the evening shift, and he'd sit in that ticket office (none of the bigwigs around to object at that time of evening) and he'd watch me selling the tickets. He picked up the system in no time. Learned all the names of the places people went, kept asking his mother to point them out on the map. Sharp as a knife, my little David.'

'That's awfully nice,' said Simon, 'provided they don't know it themselves.'

'Oh, his mother and I wouldn't have let him get uppitty. Not like those ghastly American children you see on television. Oh no—he was a sweet child, and not at all clever-clever. Everyone fell for him. Of course he looked so nice. His mother kept him spotless, and neat as a new pin. Beautiful little clothes he had, and Mary was that good at mending and patching, like we had to then. There wasn't a smarter little nipper in all Paddington. I sometimes used to watch him and his mother go off together in the morning—he used to pretend he was old enough to go to school, had his little satchel and all—and they'd go off together, him in his little grey trousers and his little blue blazer which his Mum made for him (he was that jealous of others going off dressed up for school every morning, and him not old enough)—and I tell you, just seeing them my heart leapt up with pride. It did. And if there were air raids, and he couldn't trot about like that, he used to go with his Mum down to the shelters, and he used to keep the rest of them in stitches.'

'There are some kids like that,' said Simon.

'That's right. He had all those sharp little comments and questions that kids often have, only his were that humorous! We had a dugout shelter for three or four families along Farrow Street, and he used to call it 'the burrow'. 'Can we go down the burrow?' he'd say, if there hadn't been a raid for some days. And when we were all down there, the neighbours'd say it was better than the radio—better than *Happidrome.*'

'It was a funny time for a child to grow up in,' said Simon. 'I don't remember much about it myself, except for the food.'

'No, well, little David didn't really understand, of course—took it to be normal, if you take my meaning, because he didn't remember anything else. And his mother—my Mary—she used to make a joke of it for him.

However worried she was herself, she'd always make a joke of things for him. I wasn't in the ARP then—that was later. I wasn't found fit for the army—spot of chest trouble, you know—but I did my bit on the Home Front later on. But even in those early days she was worried—naturally, because the stations were prime targets for the bombers. But she never let on to David. Never let him see how worried she was for me. What a woman, eh? A real saint!'

'What—what happened to them?'

Len's conversational flow suddenly dried up.

'I lost them.'

'In the blitz?'

Len had taken out a handkerchief, and was looking past Simon, down the ill-lit, half-empty bar. His naturally cratered face seemed about to crumble into total collapse.

'That's right. I lost them both in the air raids. It's ironic, really. Things got so bad here . . . raids every night, fires raging all around, you can't imagine what it was like . . . so Mary found this place in Sussex, not far from Brighton. I wanted my boy in the country, out of the raids. We'd often been to Brighton on holidays, and Ma had some church contacts there—fellow Baptists, you know. That's how it came about. I used to sit in the shelter in Paddington during them raids, and I used to think: well, supposing I go, I know little David will be safe . . . ' He wiped at his eyes, and Simon could see tears well up and begin to stream down his face. 'And what happened? There was this German bomber, off course for home, and he off-loaded his bombs just before he got to the Channel. There was me, went through the war with hardly a scratch, and there was little David—direct hit, killed instantly.' He sobbed. 'It's the tragedy of my life. I still can't bear to think about it. I tell you, I haven't been the same man since I lost the two of them. Not the same man at all.'

Simon watched horrified as the tears coursed down the man's hollow cheeks, unstoppable, overflowing. He felt in his stomach a heave of repulsion for the man who could cry

so convincingly for an imaginary grief, who could act out
sorrow in so abandoned a fashion when he had merely been
retelling a fantasy. For surely it was not possible that Len
was uninvolved in the disappearance of his son? Surely it
was not possible that he had been fed a fake story? Yet the
sobs that were racking his body were so heartfelt that Simon
did, just for a moment, wonder whether Len Simmeter
might not actually believe the story he had just told.

Later that evening Simon sat up writing in his notebooks,
trying to put down every tittle of information he had gleaned
from Len, and trying to recapture, when possible, Len's
own words. Sometimes as he wrote he seemed to feel a
twinge of memory: those little grey trousers; that blue blazer.
But short grey trousers and blue blazers were common
enough features of an English childhood. How could one
distinguish memory from wishful self-deception? Even the
things he was sure he remembered—the train arriving at
Yeasdon Station, for example—had become hardened in his
mind into a sort of snapshot, something he could flip through
his mind to, at will. Did he remember? Or did he just
remember that he had once remembered? Tentatively,
aware of the pitfalls, he headed a page of his notebook
'Memories', and collected everything from the beginning
that could possibly come under that heading. The notebooks, he was pleased to realize, were at last beginning to
assume a more solid, fleshed-out form.

  That night he had a dream that he had not had for many
years. The dream was a violent one, and he lay beneath the
sheet in the warm night air threshing and tossing about,
trying to wrestle himself back to wakefulness, but sinking
back over and over again into a dim struggle of black shapes.
Those shapes could not be seen clearly, but he knew they
were a man and a woman. There were cries, sobbing, and
there were shouted threats and insults. And there were
blows. Not at first, but soon: repeated blows. Sometimes the
people and the cries seemed to fade, but always it came

back: the insults, the sobs, the struggle. He was conscious there was another reality to return to, and he struggled to rise to the surface, but he always sank back down—deeper, deeper, the cries more intolerably urgent. Though he could not identify the shapes, he knew that the other he, the smaller he of his dream, could have identified them, knew what they were fighting about. Though the blows were never aimed at him, they were *about* him. So it was a fight he was witnessing, but also one in which—small, helpless as he was—he was involved. Responsible. Someone was being mistreated because of him.

When he finally fought his way back to wakefulness he was no longer small and helpless, but his chest, his back and his forehead were wet with sweat, and he felt as though he had spent the night wrestling under the sea with some dark aquatic monster with numberless entwining tentacles that choked and fettered him.

After some hesitation he entered this dream in his notebook under 'Memories'.

CHAPTER 9

One area of bafflement left by his heart-to-heart with Len was unexpectedly illuminated for Simon before the end of the week.

He had been given the job of entertaining and showing round the Zoo a visitor of no great importance—a member of the scientific staff of the zoo at Cracow. As a rule at that time the Polish government allowed outside their borders only emissaries or delegates of the most dreary party-line respectability, but this man had unexpectedly turned out to be jolly, well-informed and inquisitive, so that once Simon and he had found ways of getting round the various linguistic trip-wires which such encounters entail, they got on very well. Simon lunched him moderately lavishly at the Zoo

restaurant, and around half past two said that he'd take
him back to his hotel.

'Is little 'otel in Paddington,' said his guest. 'Is no foreign
currencies for better.'

So Simon found himself once more in Paddington. By the
time he had paid off the taxi, in a dreary little side street
ten minutes from the station, the afternoon was as good as
gone. He toyed with the idea of going to have another look
at Farrow Street, but he gave up the idea: there was no
longer any point in trying to gain admittance, even if he
could think up an excuse, and the exterior had certainly
yielded up all its secrets. From neighbours he might, eventually, be able to prise more, supposing any still remained
who had been there in the Simmeters' time, but would he
get anything from them that he had not got already from
Len or his mother? One other area of investigation, the
Baptist church, it would be best to embark upon on a
Sunday: Baptist churches in the suburbs of London were
not likely even to be open on a Friday afternoon.

So Simon began making his way towards the Underground at the main line station, desultorily, hoping for
memories or for a flash of inspiration from the ethos of the
place. So indefinite were his intentions that he had walked
past the Paddington Library and had done no more than
register that that was what it was, when it struck him that
a library in Paddington would be the very place to look for
a notice of his birth. He had vaguely intended one day to
cross the river and look it up at Somerset House, but
the Simmeters, pillars of the church, would surely have
announced it in some local newspaper. The actual date of
his birth was no very urgent matter for him—he was happy
enough to celebrate it as the day he had arrived in
Yeasdon—but it was a way of passing the afternoon, and a
way of getting a whiff of the period when he was born.

The day he arrived in Yeasdon was May 10th, 1941. He
had generally been said then to be about five. The likeliest
period for his birth, then, seemed to be the second half of

1935, or some time in 1936. Up in the Reference Library on the first floor the attendant was very helpful. There was no doubt, she said, that the most widely distributed local newspaper at that time was the *West London Recorder*. Oh yes, the files were easily accessible. Lots of local people, and historians, consulted them. Paddington had been a very lively, mixed community at the time, and its history had many aspects that interested sociologists and social historians. In a matter of minutes Simon was seated at a desk with two large and unwieldy volumes, containing all the copies of the paper for the relevant years.

The *West London Recorder* was a lugubrious paper by the standards of the 'sixties (when the slide towards tabloid hysteria was already well under way), but once Simon got used to the look of it he found it admirably set out for his purposes. The announcements of births, marriages and deaths were almost invariably on page five, opposite the main news page. The news, in the early summer of '35, when Simon started his search, was much taken up with celebrations of the Royal Jubilee. Preparations, decorations, official committees and planned festivities were reported and commented on in laborious detail. Pictures of King George V—dignified, sick-looking, slightly bemused—were printed on the slightest, or no, pretext. But this was May—too early, Simon thought, and he merely did a lightning-quick check through the advertised births. The unusualness of the name Simmeter was again a blessing. Simon could flick from one week's issue to the next in no time, even though he also took a side glance for the name Spurling. In August 1935 he did in fact find the name Spurling: Thomas James Spurling, who had died on the 23rd, aged seventy-six, and mourned by children Alice, Arthur, Henry, Enid and Mary. Simon noted down the names, and all the details that seemed relevant, in the notebooks that he took everywhere in his briefcase, away from the prying interest of the Simmeters. Elsewhere in the same issue, which he examined with special care, he found

a small news item which brought with it a little more sense
of the personality of the man:

> The death of Thomas James Spurling will be greatly
> mourned by the congregation of the Meachin Road Bap-
> tist Church. For many years Thomas Spurling was one
> of the churchwardens, a leader of the temperance group,
> and a pillar of the Sunday School. A man of fine presence
> and strong principles, his rich bass voice was an asset to
> the choir, and his solo performances at church functions
> gave great pleasure to many, even when he was into his
> seventies. Mr Spurling was born in Dumfries, and will be
> much missed by family, friends, and the Baptist congre-
> gation.

So it would seem that his grandfather had died around the
time that he, Simon, was born. It was a pity he would
apparently not have seen him as a baby, for Thomas James
Spurling sounded like the sort of man who would take pride
in grandchildren, particularly male grandchildren. Perhaps
he had known of the approaching birth. Since Mary was
the youngest child, and since he guessed from photographs
that she was not young when she married Len, it was not
surprising that his grandfather had not lived to see his
Simmeter grandson's childhood.

Simon noted down the further details from the news
paragraph, and in the red ballpoint which he used for further
lines of inquiry he suggested: 'older members of the present
Baptist congregation?' and 'other members of the Spurling
family?' Staunch churchmen and churchwomen of Scottish
extraction lived long—lived to an abstemious and censorious
old age. Then Simon went back to flicking through the
Recorders, week by week, in search of some notice of his own
birth. That death notice for Thomas Spurling, as well as
the news item, suggested that the Spurlings at least were a
family that set some store by their position in the community, that felt the need to memorialize publicly the

 additions, alignments and subtractions that occurred to the main familiar body. Perhaps the Spurling sense of their own worth had had to triumph over the innate Simmeter love of secrecy.

But it was when he got to the autumn of that year that he made a discovery that dwarfed the trivial matter of his own birth date. Starting on the issue for October 13th he turned as usual to page five, with hardly more than a glance at the news on page six. But the glance was enough. He swung his head back and peered close. In the centre of the page was a news picture of Mosley's blackshirts marching through Paddington. On they advanced towards the camera, right arms raised, at once menacing and slightly ridiculous: clerks and retired army men, thugs and respectable householders, the prosperous, the unemployed and the unemployable—that motley, unanalysable *olla podrida* that has made up all the movements, the factions and the splinters of Britain's right-wing activity over the past sixty years. And on the left of the picture—black-shirted, black-booted like the rest, his hand raised above his shoulder in salute—was Len Simmeter.

Was it really him? Simon bent down over the hefty volume and looked closely. It *must* be. The same sunken cheeks, the old-young face, the mean eyes, just as he had seen them in the wedding photograph. And just as he had watched the older version, sitting opposite him in the Colonel Monk. Len was of the kind whose face sets young, whom age and experience modify or imprint deeper, but never change. There might conceivably be doubles of Len, fortuitous replicas outside the family (for it was a face of no distinction or grace); but fortuitous replicas in the Paddington area would surely be carrying coincidence too far. Simon sat back, contemplative, in his chair.

Now he had seen that picture, now he had learnt of Len's grubby little commitment, so many other things began to make sense. That insistence on bringing up the 'crooked nose' people on the Zoo board. The reference was an echo

of so many jaded political battle cries—to the wrong people
being in charge. What, Simon wondered, had been the
precise nature of Len's trouble at work that the girl next
door had mentioned—trouble that had led to stoppages and
the threat of a strike? He remembered Len's tired references
to the law and order problem, and the fact that (he said) it
had only cropped up in the last ten or fifteen years. 'We all
know who's to blame,' he had said.

Simon was willing to bet that behind the troubles at the
Angel there lurked Len's racial attitudes: that the Jew-baiter
of the 'thirties had become the immigrant-baiter of the
'sixties.

Suddenly he remembered, with shame, that he had referred to some of the Zoo board as 'rich as Jews'. It was a
casual, rural phrase he'd picked up as a child, but as stupid
a thing to say as he could imagine, particularly since several
of the board *were* Jews. In the musty privacy of the Paddington Reference Library Simon blushed. It was that casual
phrase, of course, that had started things off, had made Len
Simmeter imagine an affinity between them. That was the
reason for all the oblique probing and hinting that Len had
indulged in at the Colonel Monk; and that was the basis for
the feeling he had got that he, rather than Len, was under
investigation. Len was sounding him out to recruit him—not
necessarily for any organization, but to join him in his
nasty little racial antagonisms, to settle down to sessions of
like-minded jeremiads about the state of the world and
the inborn inferiority of certain sections of it. Simon felt
demeaned.

His interest in the *West London Recorder* now focused itself
on the news pages rather than on page five. It was clear that
the Mosleyites were active and relatively successful in the
Paddington area in the mid-'thirties. It was not, in fact, the
only Fascist organization that was flourishing there, though
it was certainly the largest. Simon got the impression that
as the librarian had said, Paddington had been a very mixed
area, full of life and interest and contrasts, but providing

the basis for the sort of antagonisms on which a movement like Mosley's British Union could flourish. There were mentions of public meetings, party meetings, outdoor demonstrations, and marches. If the health of a political movement could be measured by its success in keeping in the public eye, then the Mosleyites were thriving.

The news items, though, were mostly fairly small: the owner of the *West London Recorder* was obviously no Rothermere, finding the new movement attractive enough to flirt with and flatter. Still, however much the owner or editor might have disliked them, they were news, and they capitalized on their newsworthiness. They were helped by world events which impinged on the heterogeneous community of Paddington. The Italians in Abyssinia, Hitler occupying the Rhineland, the rumours of show trials in Russia—all these could be commented on by a political group which took its tone from the masterly self-publicist who led them. At last, in July 1936, Simon came upon the name he wanted. BRITISH UNION WELCOMES ARMY COUP IN SPAIN said the headline. Underneath was a statement from Leonard Simmeter, Deputy Chairman of the Paddington Branch, in which he expressed the view that Red Chaos was at an end in Spain, and that law, order and a respect for authority would now be restored. Simon could almost picture the young Len rubbing his hands as he expressed this slightly premature view.

As 1936 took its course, the tempo of Mosleyite activity hotted up. There came through their demonstrations and statements a feeling of sailing with the wind, a gloating anticipation of future triumphs: they had seen the future, and it was theirs. The Abdication Crisis threw them slightly, and they resorted as so often, to talk of 'conspiracy'. But for the rest there was a tang of confidence, of black-and-white certainties: brutality of words mirrored a brutality of action; bully-boy tactics were resorted to without apology. In December there was another picture: a large meeting with Mosley as speaker. If Simon had not seen the earlier picture he would not have noticed Len, but there he was, seated at his Leader's left hand, gazing up at him with awe. The week after there was a report of a hundred-strong contingent from the area joining the rest of London's Unionists for a march through the East End. And the week after that there was comment in the leader column, expressing the view that the breaking of windows in Jewish-owned shops and factories, the daubing of anti-Semitic slogans, was un-English and intolerable in a civilized community. It voiced the hope that such excesses of a movement 'which includes many men of goodwill' would not spread to the Paddington area. It seemed a vain hope.

When Simon looked at his watch it was close on six. He had not found out the date of his birth, but what he had found was much more valuable: he had unearthed the clue to Len Simmeter, had caught the flavour of the atmosphere in which Len lived at the time of his own birth and childhood. Simon pushed the heavy volumes aside and walked out of the library, into the present-day world of Beatlemania, of David Frost and Millicent Martin, of racial tensions, the aftermath of sex scandals, and people still having great hopes of Harold Wilson.

That Friday was one of the turning-points in Simon's search. No sooner had one important piece in the puzzle been given its place than a new avenue for investigation opened itself up for him. When he arrived back at Miswell Terrace, having snatched a quick meal at an ABC, a fair-haired woman was turning into the gate of No. 25 a few yards ahead of him. By a stroke of luck she stood on the steps fumbling for her keys.

So far all Simon had seen of Connie Simmeter had been the fading fair hair of the top of her head. Though she was regular in her time of leaving in the mornings—so regular that Simon had considered chiming in with her, even though that would have meant arriving at work much too early—her time of arrival home was much more erratic. On one or two occasions it had been after the other two had gone to bed. Now, without premeditation, they had coincided.

'Let me help you,' said Simon.

'Oh, how kind. I know I *have* the key, but you know women and their handbags! You must be the young gentleman from the top floor. I've heard so much about you.'

Close up, Connie presented something of a contrast to the other two Simmeters Simon had met. There was a superficial smartness about her that was certainly quite foreign to them. She was fifty or so, running to plumpness, but the flesh was apparently well-corseted, and the whalebone-enclosed package was clad in a simple, rather anonymous navy suit. Nylon-stockinged, high-heeled, well-manicured, she was a 'fifties rather than a 'sixties figure. She had a conscious air of having a position to maintain: face recently repowdered, hair in place. For some years yet she would be able to sustain the reputation of an attractive woman. What could be her profession? Manager of a small shop, top-grade secretary with a not-too-reliable firm? There was a compliance, an anxiety to please about her: the sort of woman who might, for a consideration, show her suspender-belt to a gentleman whom suspender-belts excited.

'You're Simon Cutheridge, I know. I'm Constance. The family call me Connie, but I don't let anyone else use that.'

'Constance has a certain—air to it, though,' suggested Simon.

'It does, doesn't it? Whereas Connie has no style at all. I can't get them out of it, though. That's the trouble of living with your family: they never let you grow up, never realize you've become someone else.'

She smiled a brilliant, practised smile. Her eyes had been artificially rendered more liquid and sparkling, and they obligingly sparkled. A woman used to attracting, now anxious to attract.

'Luckily I've always been Simon, even to my family. Nobody uses Sim these days, do they? What about your brother, though? I expect you call him Len, but perhaps somewhere there's a Leonard struggling to get out.'

She giggled, and switched on the brilliant smile again.

'I'm sure there is. Though whether as Leonard he'd be any more ... Well, you don't want to hear our family problems, do you? I hear you're from the West Country.'

'Down in that direction.'

'Such a lovely part of England. I love touring round, don't you? Just seeing new places. Now Len, he's hardly moved out of London in years. And Mother—well, as you've seen, Mother's hardly movable these days, but even before that she never went in much for travelling. I'm afraid I'm not like that. I did the West Country with a friend.' She released another liquid, rehearsed smile, to leave him in no doubt of the sex of the friend. 'We had lovely weather, and I tell you it was idyllic. That's the only word for it. And then there's Scotland. Skye, now—isn't Skye lovely? And North Wales! I love Betws-y-Coed. Oh yes—' she let out a brassy laugh —'I've been around!'

They were in the hallway now, and Simon tried desperately to prolong the conversation. It was less of a problem with Connie than with the others, since she was in no way loath to chat. She had perched herself on the little hall table as if she expected to be there for some time.

'Do you work in this area?' asked Simon.

'This dump? You must be joking. I work in the Strand. Peter Lewis's, you know. I manage the glove and handbag department. It's a very good job. Nice type of clientele—lots of them regulars: people from the country like yourself, clergymen's wives, that sort of thing. It's not quite what I planned, but I mustn't grumble.'

'What did you plan, then?'

'Oh, you know: something with a bit more style. Perhaps something rather more intellectual. But then there were—things: it wasn't so easy getting an education in those days; my husband died very young; and then there was the war ... I don't know, I suppose I let myself get into a bit of a rut. So here I am—' she tried out a brave-little-woman face, but it suited her less well than the man-charmer—'still stuck at home with all the old familiar faces!'

'You never wanted to take a flat on your own?'

'Oh, I've tried that. Can't say I liked it. Too much like hard work. You can say what you like about independence, but it can't compete with a hot meal ready for you when you get home. I like things done for me—always have. If I have a gentleman friend, I like *him* to invite *me* out. That's how it should be, I think. If he knows he can always come round to yours, he starts regarding you as a bit on the side. No—living at home really works out very well.' She laughed again, rather bitterly. 'Even if the company *at* home is nothing to *write* home about.'

'I've no brothers or sisters,' said Simon, 'so I can't guess what it'd be like. I'd have thought it would be difficult if you'd been married, as you have—and of course as Len has too.'

A veil seemed to fall across Connie's liquid eyes. She seemed to decide not to let her chattiness take her too far, and got up from her perch. From this point on she seemed to take care what she was saying.

'Oh yes, we've both been married, though I don't use my married name any longer. Len was as unlucky as I was, in a different way. He lost his wife in the raids, you know. And then his little boy. You might say he has a right to be bitter, though I never remember him much different. It's no good moping, is it? That's not how I've lived my life. Got to keep your chin up, that's what I say.' She squared her shoulders and produced a brave smile. 'I'd better go in, or that precious pair will start wondering. You must come and have a meal with us some time—if I can persuade Mother to cook anything worth eating. Well—'bye for now!'

She took her keys from her handbag, and let herself into the ground-floor lair. It occurred to Simon to wonder whether she had sensed him coming up behind her in the street, and had only pretended to have lost her keys. There

were few enough young lodgers in the Terrace, and she had
no doubt been given a description of him.

   He did not like her, he decided. There was about her a
torpor—physical, certainly, but moral as well. She would
lie, he felt sure, casually, for no purpose but to make a better
impression. When he came later in the evening to enter up
a résumé of the conversation with Connie, something struck
him that had not done so at the time. There seemed to be
a discrepancy between Connie's account and Len's of the
tragedy of Len's married life. He went back over the conversation in his mind, and then tried to set down that portion
as exactly as he could. Yes, there was a discrepancy, at
least by implication. Because Len had implied—though not
stated—that his wife and his little boy had both been killed
in the same air raid. Whereas Connie had implied—again,
not stated—that these were two separate blows. About the
little boy, at least, he was sure that both were telling lies;
but over the years their stories seemed to have diverged.
Perhaps in the course of time those lies, that divergence,
might be a stepping-stone to the truth.

CHAPTER 10

So after all it had to be Paddington again, Simon concluded.
It was Paddington that held those clues to his past that
would not easily be screwed out of the inhabitants of Miswell
Terrace. But was there anything to be done there beyond a
further trudge through newspapers? What Simon wanted to
hear about was not Len the Mosleyite spokesman, but Len
the family fascist. And yet, the more he acclimatized himself
to the Paddington of the 'sixties, the more he wondered
whether it had any real links with the Paddington of the
'thirties. Many of the respectable lower middle-class houses
had become one-night cheap hotels (or establishments cater-
ing for even shorter stays). It was an area of mean bedsitters,

desperate shifts to ward off destitution, of petty crime, prostitution and racial tensions. But surely somewhere still there were people with memories, somewhere some sense of continuity back to the Depression?

His first expedition was in the nature of a reconnaissance. After work one day he roamed the streets like a cat, first those around the Station, then further afield. The atmosphere of the area he was already prepared for. It lurked behind the greying net curtains, it rose like a steam from the shabby macs: an atmosphere of meanness and failure. And above all of loneliness, and the festering bitterness of loneliness. It was an area of fragments—each bedsitter held one, and the fragments nursed their solitudes and never came together.

Seedy was too kind to describe the neighbourhood: it was decayed. On the walls slogans were scrawled in white paint: KILL THE TORIES or FUCK WILSON. The racial slogans were similarly basic: WOGS OUT or CASTRATE ALL NIGS. Simon could imagine the slogan painters —sidling out, alone, after dark, viewing their work with secret satisfaction the next day. He went into a pub and started chatting to people—dispirited people, all of whom had moved there last year, or last week, who hoped to move out next year, next week, definitely before long. Paddington, for them, was not a community: it was streets, houses—or, more essentially, *rooms*. Some were even less permanent: Simon bought a pint for one old cadger who turned out to be a semi-derelict, on his way from Sidcup, and on his way back there, he said. Paddington's present seemed a guttering, feeble flame; its past dead beyond recall.

Out in the streets again the area began to split itself up a little for him, to acquire individual characteristics. This one was mostly small hotels, this one bedsitters, this other one still precariously middle-class and residential. Here were Italian voices, rich Italian smells, while elsewhere were Indians, Indian smells, turbans. In one area, five or six streets away from Farrow Street, Simon noticed that the racial sloganizing was especially thick—violent, semi-

literate, obsessive. Yet as he dawdled round it he could not
see that it was a section with a high concentration of
immigrants. Odd. Then he noticed that political activity
of a kind seemed to flourish here. Small notices, crudely
duplicated, were pasted on to the edge of hoardings, on
empty houses, displayed in the windows of small shops.
The League of Empire Loyalists summoned the citizens of
Paddington from their bedsitters for AN EXPRESSION
OF PUBLIC CONCERN at the Morton Hall—that was
three days ago. The National Front announced a demonstration STOP IMMIGRATION NOW, starting at the
Town Hall. They were preparing the ground with a rash of
small stickers: IS IT WRONG TO WANT TO STAY
WHITE? and DO YOU REMEMBER WHEN BRITAIN
WAS BRITISH?

There was a third organization soliciting support from
the people of Paddington—for the Right would not be the
Right (any more than the Left would be the Left) if it did
not split asunder into myriad groups, sniping at each other,
proclaiming their own ideological purity, displaying all the
self-righteousness of the politically unco' guid. This group
called itself The British Citizens' Army. Its posters, small
and messy as the rest, managed to include some article of
military significance—a peaked cap, a rifle, even a black
military boot. From the downward stroke of the initial B in
their title a Union Jack fluttered. The wording of their
posters and stickers was suitably aggressive: 'fight', 'struggle', 'hit back' featured prominently, usually capitalized.
Some of the aggression and racial viciousness had a pathetic
ring to it, like a child who mistreats his puppy because he
himself is not getting enough attention. Many of the posters
announced their next meeting—August 2nd, also at the
Morton Hall (whose owners, presumably, were broad-
minded, or something). Simon found one of their notices in
the door of a newsagent/tobacconist that stayed open late.
He pushed open the door and went in.

'I saw your notice in the window,' he said, as he slowly

fished for the change for twenty Kensitas. 'About the British
Citizens' Army meeting.'

'Not my notice, mate. One of me customers.'

'What sort of a bunch are they?'

'Search me. Bloke who give it to me's not much more'n
a kid. He's a bit of a nut, if you ask me, but he gets his fags
here regular, so I couldn't say no. The 'all's round the
corner, if you're interested.'

'Oh, I don't know that I'd go that far.'

''Course, they've got a point . . . '

'You think so, do you? Will you go to the meeting?'

'Don't be barmy. They're a lot of weirdos.'

His combination of cynicism and sloth seemed a very
British defence against political extremists.

In deciding on the Citizens' Army as the first subject for
his investigation of Paddington's fringe Right, Simon was
mainly influenced by the fact that they had a meeting
coming up in a few days' time. Perhaps men—and women,
of course—of Len's generation were more likely to let themselves be clasped in the semi-respectable embrace of The
League of Empire Loyalists. Others, presumably had simply
stayed loyal to Mosley, and many more, of course, would
have joined the Conservative Party. But the Citizens' Army,
in addition to their forthcoming meeting, had a sort of showy
nastiness about it, and Simon thought it might be not unlike
the Mosley movement of thirty years before, and appeal to
a rather similar mob.

In the interval before the night of the meeting he gave
some thought as to how he should dress. He could well
imagine the sort of pseudo-military gear that would be on
display at the meeting, as well as the mothballed treasures
of the war veterans. In the end he decided against any
attempt to play along with that kind of performance: it
would go too obviously against his whole personality. He
compromised by having an unusually short haircut.

On the evening of August 2nd he did not go home after
work, but had a meal in a little Italian restaurant in Baker

Street, and then strolled along towards Paddington. It was a quarter to seven before he came to the area where the posters and stickers had proliferated, and he found the Morton Hall without difficulty. It was a square, drab building of no particular religious affiliation and no architectural distinction at all. He had time in hand, and he wandered round the adjacent streets, sniffing in vain for signs of approaching excitements. He bought a pineapple and pistachio concoction from an ice-cream van on the corner, and stood against a wall licking it and waiting for developments.

It wasn't until a quarter past seven that first one motorcycle, then another and another, zoomed up the road from the direction of the Station and swerved flashily in outside the hall, revving their engines several times as some kind of demonstration, then parking neatly in line. The machines were loud rather than powerful, and so were their riders. They took off their helmets, stood talking for a moment on the pavement, then in semi-unison they about-turned and marched shoulder to shoulder into the hall. The effect was both risible and sinister at the same time.

Now there were more coming: elderly people, almost all men, with a sort of seedy respectability—suits, collar and tie, raincoats over their arm, but almost all their clothing cheap, dubiously clean. More motor-cyclists arrived, and other teenagers who obviously hoped to graduate to motorcycledom. The only young women were hangers-on of these, but there was the odd middle-aged woman of the sort who would complain about the smell of curries cooking, or proclaim their unwillingness to go out after dark.

It was now twenty-five past. An elderly Hillman Minx drove up and parked a hundred yards away. A podgy man in his thirties got out and bustled self-importantly round to the back of the hall. Simon swallowed the last of his cornet, wet his handkerchief to wipe his hands, then sauntered across the street and into the hall.

The first thing that happened was that a cyclostyled pamphlet was thrust into his hand by one of the motor cycling youths, who was standing by the door.

'Read this, mate, and see what we're up against,' the blotchy-faced young man said, with some relish.

It was not necessary to read the pamphlet to see that the posters in public places in fact represented the Citizens' Army respectable face. The pamphlet was vile: the hoariest racial myths presented as news items, the silliest theories of racial purity reduced to tabloid form—the whole punctuated by triple exclamation marks, and disgracefully spelt. Simon refrained from crumpling it in his fist. He glanced at it with an appearance of interest, then put it in his pocket.

Surveying the audience from the back of the hall, it was easier to feel pity than anger. The young men in particular seemed anachronistic survivals from the era of depression: so many seemed undernourished, or the victims of the diseases of poverty, that they looked like Dotheboys Hall grown up. Tight jeans exposed pitifully thin flanks, matchstick arms protruded from T-shirts, the close-cut hair made them look wretched rather than manly. Some wore army tunics, all attempted a swagger, without the physical means that swaggers are built on.

But it was the older members of the audience that interested Simon. Most of the young men sitting in the body of the hall were sad, lonely individuals, each sitting apart, with shabby shoes, shiny flannel trousers and synthetic shirts. One guessed they would smell of underclothes washed in the handbasins of their bedsitters. Many of the older members of the audience looked to be their equivalents: they were there for somewhere to go, as in winter they would huddle in the reading rooms of public libraries. What Simon looked for was not someone sunk in apathy or isolation, but someone with commitment.

Half way down the hall his eyes rested on a man of fifty or so, seated forward in his chair, his shoulders tensed to expectancy. This man was not, like the rest, simply *there:* he was there and waiting to get something from it. Simon strolled down the centre aisle. When he got closer he read

on the man's face a certain hunger, an intense eagerness
that he seemed to recognize: he had seen it on Len
Simmeter's face at moments when they talked in the pub.
There was a sense in this man of a craving for illicit excitements, and not the usual excitements craved by shabby men
in their fifties. Simon suddenly made up his mind, and sat
himself down on the gangway seat beside him.

The man first turned round, surprised, as if interrupted
in the middle of some intense private meditation. But he
was not hostile. On the contrary, he actually spoke.

'Good evening, young man.'

'Good evening.'

'Never seen you at one of these meetings before. New to
the area? It's nice to see a respectable type here. There's
too many of these scruffies—' he waved his arm in the
direction of the motor-cycle boys—'begging their pardon.
They haven't got a brain in their heads. They're just here
for the kicks.'

And was he, Simon wondered, here for the intellectual
content? He sank into a predetermined pose of simple-
minded, cliché-ridden enthusiasm.

'It takes all sorts.'

'Oh, right. Too right, young man. A movement can find
uses for all manner of people. It's not a bad audience, is
it?' He gazed around the Hall, which was half to two-thirds
full. Not at all a bad turn-out, though a sad little assembly
they looked. 'Not bad at all. I don't know about you, but
I've sensed for a long time a change in the wind. You might
say people are beginning to sense The Danger. It's taken
time. Ten years ago you'd have hardly got a soul to a meeting
like this. But the message is getting through. Notting Hill
made people think—and Sir Oswald, bless him, standing in
Kensington. That did a power of good. We're getting a lot
of young folk, just as we used to, but we want the right
sort, young men like yourself. What brought you tonight, I
wonder?'

'Oh—er—well—' Simon, stammering, entered reluc-

tantly that area between truth and lies—'well, my father
was always very interested. He . . . he didn't live here, but
he had contacts with people in the area. And as I'd just
moved here . . . '

'I see. Was it the British Union of Fascists by any chance?'

'Yes, it was. Before the war. He mentioned a chap called
Len Simmeter.'

'That's right. I knew Len. Very enthusiastic indeed, Len
was.'

It was, frustratingly, at this point that the proceedings
began to get under way. The first to speak was one of the
older-looking of the motor-cycle mob—the only one with
the bulk and muscle to look at all impressive. Simon soon
realized that he was the warm-up man for The Leader, to
whom he repeatedly referred. As oratory his style left almost
everything to be desired, but it had a sort of gut-appeal:
he was at one with his audience in his background, his
deprivations, his obsessions. By the end of his speech, which
Simon found so loathsome he felt as if cockroaches were
crawling up his neck, he was getting little bursts of clapping,
and elderly 'hear, hears'.

'Not a bad lad,' opined Simon's neighbour tolerantly. 'Be
useful in a barney. Just doesn't have the style.'

When he had ranted to a halt, it was the turn of The
Leader. The Leader had not until now graced the platform.
His entry was the occasion for some embryonic ceremonial
—should the movement flourish, Simon felt sure, the ceremonial would augment itself to keep pace with its
prosperity. As it was, his coming on to the stage was marked
by most of the younger members of the audience, and a few
of the older ones, rising to their feet and saluting. The
Leader was the pudgy man whom Simon had seen outside,
now wearing some kind of simple shirt-tunic and breeches,
and flanked on stage by two bovver-boys wearing the kind
of army uniform that might have graced an amateur pro-
duction of *The Love of Four Colonels*.

He was not physically impressive, this Leader. When he

began speaking, however, it was clear that he was in
different league from the warm-up boy. His voice was richer
though still with a proletarian twang. His sentences cohered
were prepared and rehearsed. His oratorical style was pat
terned on Mussolini's rather than Hitler's, so it aroused
fewer unhappy memories: the English have always had
slightly tender spot in their hearts for the Italian posture
and while they would never have made him their leader
they might well have put him in charge of British Rail
If the content of the Leader's speech was similar to th
earlier one, here the rampant racism was refined, filled
out with historical and philosophical references, making
more subtle and insidious appeal. His audience, he seemed
to say, were intelligent and educated people like himself
and what they all believed had respectable intellectua
roots.

To come to such a meeting (without any intention c
breaking it up) was something few of Simon's generation c
intellectuals could expect to do. He found he could shut hi
ears to the content of the speech, and merely pay attentior
to the sound, to the shaping of the arguments, the oratorica
tricks, the cunning of the allusions, the oblique flattery c
the direct appeals. It was a technique of listening Simor
later applied to Party Political Broadcasts, and that perhap
explains why he sometimes never bothered to vote at all ir
elections. Judged this way, the man had what it takes. Th
man in the seat next to Simon agreed.

'He's a man with a future,' he whispered in Simon's ear
'Next to Sir Oswald, you won't find a speaker in Englan
today to beat him.'

The meeting drew to a close with singing. The motor
cycle boys began it—a fine, surging, thrusting melod
with stampings of the feet. Simon could well imagine th
Wehrmacht singing it as they forged into Brussels o
Athens. Later they interspersed such numbers with Englis
songs, and the meeting ended with 'I Vow to Thee, M
Country'

'Well, that's the sort of meeting that really makes you feel better,' said Simon's neighbour.

'It certainly gave us plenty to think about,' murmured Simon.

'At last the message is getting through,' said the older man, his voice betraying the same sort of desperation an ageing British Communist feels after decades of banging his head against a brick wall. '*At last!* People are beginning to sit up and think. Marvellous, i'n't it, that we have to have half a million Aliens in our midst before the British will do that!'

The meeting was breaking up. The Leader had come off the platform, and was pretending to be an ordinary mortal. He was mingling with his audience, shaking their hands, and hoping they'd come again—very much in the manner of an Anglican clergyman. One or two ladies asked him questions beginning 'What are you going to do about . . . ?' He answered as if he expected to be in power tomorrow. Simon kept close to his new friend as they made for the door and out into the street. Outside dusk had gathered, lights were lit, and the shabby houses had acquired a sort of romance.

'I feel a lot better for that,' said the older man, as if he had swallowed a dose of patent medicine. 'Feel like a cup of coffee, young man?'

'I wouldn't mind at all,' said Simon, disguising his joy.

'There's a late night place just around the corner. My name's Al Needham, by the way. I'm glad I met up with you. It's a real tonic when a respectable young chap like yourself takes an interest, because we do get a few of the other kind, even in our set-up.'

'Your set-up?'

'I'm not a member of this bunch. I've stayed loyal to Sir Oswald, God bless him. But what I think is, we're all in this together, all right-thinking citizens, all fighting shoulder to shoulder. So I come along and give them my support.' He needs a frequent jab in the arm, Simon thought, and he goes to the meetings of any group that can give him one.

Al pushed open the door of a café and marched up to the counter. 'Two coffees, please.' It was the traditional greasy, dreary, uncaring British café—the sort of place that has given the British pub its reputation for cosiness. The coffee was boiling milk poured over coffee essence. Round the tables old men and women dallied over their dregs, some reading the evening paper for the third time, some gazing in front of them, unseeing. Simon and Al Needham collected their cups and made for a table by the window.

'Yes, Mosley's my man,' said Al, stirring his coffee with all the appearance of expecting to enjoy it. 'And I don't doubt he'll have worthy successors. I've spent my life recruiting Youth to the Union, and what we want now is a few more clean-limbed, thinking young people, like yourself.'

Simon thought he had never been made to sound more dreadful.

'Was it you recruited Len Simmeter?' he asked.

'Oh no—we're much of an age, as far as I remember. In fact, I joined later—round about 'thirty-three, and he'd been in for a couple of years then. He'd been on a trip to Italy, seen good old Musso. So he went in with Sir Oswald right from the moment he split with the Labour Party. Matter of fact, it was at a meeting where he was one of the speakers that I joined the Union—rather like you tonight, young man.'

'Yes,' said Simon, with what he felt to be transparently false enthusiasm. 'It must have been a tremendously exciting time, the 'thirties.'

'Oh, it was, it was,' said Al, who had finished stirring his coffee and was now licking the spoon. 'You should have seen the support we had! And the speakers! Lots of your intellectuals—Harold Nicolson, Christopher Isherwood—all sorts. They didn't stay, of course—those brains types haven't got the staying power of us common-or-garden types. But what a time it was!'

'Was Len Simmeter a good speaker at meetings? You say he more or less recruited you.'

'Well, he was and he wasn't. More the sort for leading the marches. But he made a good warm-up speaker, like that young bloke tonight. And now and then he could really surpass himself. I remember one meeting—much later it was, just before the war—and he was telling this big open-air meeting that you'd got to break the power of the Jews (it was all Jews then, not the coloureds), and he went down into the crowd and he took up his little boy—the apple of his eye, he was, and hardly more than a babby—and he held him up and he shouted, "Until you smash Jew power, this country'll never be safe for your kids and my kids." There was a great roar at that. They loved it.'

'I bet they did,' said Simon. He searched his memory for an image of a sea of faces, seen from small eyes above a crowd, but his public debut had left no picture on his mind.

'His wife didn't like it. I was standing just by her when he came and got the nipper, and she didn't like it at all. But she wasn't the type to say. Just sort of screwed up her lips.'

'She died, didn't she? My father mentioned she died quite young.'

'That's right. Died in the blitz. That would have been 'forty-one, I'd guess. I didn't have much contact with Len by then. Naturally we was both lying low.'

'Lying low?'

"'Case they interned us, of course. Like they did Sir Oswald. Just like Them, isn't it, to intern the most patriotic of the lot. Gerry Forbes—that was Len's immediate superior in Paddington—he got taken. And one or two who were with A. S. Leese's lot—the Imperial Fascists, they called themselves. So during 'forty and 'forty-one we was both lying very low indeed. And I do know that Len was taken in for questioning several times, but they always let him go. Wasn't a big enough fish, I suppose.'

'What was she like, Len's wife?'

'Very quiet sort of body. He saw to that, I shouldn't wonder—and that mother of his. Old Mrs Simmeter did a lot of work for the Union (like Sir Oswald's mother), but she wasn't what I'd call a companionable body. Len's wife was kept very much in the background. What was it Hitler said women should occupy their time with? Kitchen, children, church—something like that. Well, that was pretty much her life. Maybe she wasn't entirely with us, for all I know, but anyway Len didn't involve her in Movement activities. She adored that little boy they had. Any child she was like a protector to. She couldn't hardly bear to part from him when he had to be evacuated. Wanted him with her, yet didn't, if you follow me. Len wouldn't let her go with the boy. Thought her place was with him.'

'So the boy was evacuated, was he?'

'Oh yes, I believe so. So I was told. Somewhere in Sussex. But she stayed on, and in the end they both got their number. Her first, then him later, so far as I recall. Awful. I didn't have much contact then, as I say, but I believe it really broke Len up, losing that boy of his. He's not been the same man since.'

'You've seen him since the war, have you?'

'Oh yes. *After* the war things were very quiet for a bit. But I've seen him at party congresses and suchlike. He was active in the Kensington by-election, like I was. But he's not high up in the Party, as he might have expected. It's like he was broken, or like he'd had some big fright he never recovered from. No bounce. And you can't do anything in a movement like ours without a bit of bounce!'

'I suppose not,' said Simon.

'It's a movement that's got to appeal to the young, the virile. That's always been my job, getting the young people in. Used to get a lot of recruits out of the Scouts, the Boys' Brigade, and so on. Pity they're not flourishing like they were. Schools don't have their cadet corps either. You've got to find likely types where you can, these days.'

'Well,' said Simon, getting up, his coffee still unfinished. 'I'd better be making my way.'

Al Needham drained his cup, licked his tongue around his mouth, and stood up.

'You'll be back, won't you, young man? I say, write your name and address down for me—I've got this little notebook I keep for just such an eventuality as this.'

Simon took the dog-eared notebook, leaned over the table, and wrote in it 'Simon Thorn' and a totally fictitious address.

'Good. Excellent. I'd like you to come along to one of *our* meetings. See how they suit you. It's a more respectable set-up, ours. But we need young, bright boys like yourself—it's not every day we come across them, by Harry! You'd be getting in on the ground floor. People are beginning to think! There's an exciting time coming! Think about it, young man! I'll be in touch.'

The older man waved, and trotted off into the dark, to nourish his hopes of a new dawn and a new generation of fine, well-spoken young recruits. Simon took once more the familiar roads that led to Paddington Station.

CHAPTER 11

'I'm expecting Teddy round next week,' said Len to Simon one evening when, quite exceptionally, they met on the first-floor landing.

Simon had in fact heard Len's footsteps coming up and going into his bedroom for something, and he had chosen that time to go down to the lavatory. He had not seen Len for some time, having failed to coincide either with his morning or his evening shifts. There was a nagging feeling inside him that he needed to see Len from time to time, that he had to check his impressions of him, to see if they cohered with what he was learning about him. He is my father, he said to himself. And he added: and I want to know what he did to my mother.

So when he met Len on the first landing he stopped on the pretext of asking about the old lady. Len shook his head, with an expression of concern.

'I'm afraid she's failing,' he said. 'Very much so.' He tapped his head. 'Up here, too. Pitiful to watch. And yet she won't give up, you know. Still thinks she ought to make the decisions, like she always has. Even though she hasn't got the concentration any longer. Tragic. Still—I'm expecting Teddy round next week. That ought to perk her up a bit.'

'That's your brother, isn't it?'

'That's right. The baby of the family. Teddy always keeps people amused. It's a sort of gift—I haven't got it. I'm more the serious type. But Teddy's got it and to spare—don't know where it comes from. I hope he'll do Ma a bit of good, though I realize it can't be permanent. He'll notice the difference in her. To be perfectly frank, I can see the writing on the wall . . . '

Simon sensed a deeply buried undertone of relish.

It meant that Simon, in the next week, haunted the Colonel Monk. Teddy might not relax from his duty of cheering up the Aged P. sufficiently long to pop along there as he apparently usually did, but there again, those duties were likely to prove tiring . . . The landlord at the pub, faced with a nightly visit from Simon, did not relax from his surly gloom. In fact one evening he came close to suggesting he'd be happier if he went elsewhere.

'Seeing a lot of you lately,' he said. Casting a dispirited eye around his elderly and miserable clientèle, he added: 'Most of the young people go down the road.'

'Oh, I like a quiet pub,' said Simon.

In fact, the odd young person did come in, sometimes just to buy crisps or a pork pie, sometimes to down a single drink and then take himself out. On the Wednesday night, chirpy and glowing in the prevailing gloom, the girl from next door popped in for a bottle of stout.

'Hello,' said Simon. 'Let me buy you a drink.'

'Well, I don't know. I shouldn't. I'm getting this for my landlady—she's got one of those heavy head colds. Can't understand how anybody can drink this stuff, cold or not. I suppose she won't die if I have a quick one. I'd like a lager and lime.'

So he got her a drink, and they sat cosily together in one of the murky corners of the saloon bar, a corner where the cleaner in the morning seemed to have dumped most of what her dustpan had collected. The girl lit up the corner though, Simon thought: she was warm and quirky and funny, and vitality came crackling out of her.

'What on earth are you doing drinking in this horrible dive?' she whispered with a giggle. 'The people who come here mostly seem to be plucking up courage to end it all. The young people all go to the Jolly Beagle. It's another hundred yards down the road, but it's worth it.'

'So I've been told. But I have my reasons,' said Simon, with mock portentousness. 'You're right it's not much of a place, though. You expect spiders to come and weave webs around you if you sit here too long.'

'How's life and everything? Settling into London?'

Simon was disconcerted by the question. He had been so preoccupied that he had never asked himself that. And he'd done precious few of the things people settling into London usually do.

'I suppose so. I've been so busy I hardly know. It's always a business, getting on top of a new job.'

'What do you do?'

'I'm at the London Zoo. On the scientific staff.'

'Oh, what a smashing job. What are you doing staying in a mucky dump like Miswell Terrace? You should have a sharp little flat.'

'I have my reasons. Oh, I've said that, haven't I? Well, I expect I will be getting a flat before long. At the moment I don't get much time for looking.'

'I'm going to share a flat next year. You know, go in with two or three other girls. I'm filling in time working at a hairdresser's. But I'm going to drama school—I've got a place at the Central Academy—next year. I didn't think I was ready yet this year to get the most out of it.'

'One day I'll see your name in lights. You'd better tell me what it is or the whole effect will be lost.'

'I'm Rosemary Short. Rosie, my friends call me. And you're Simon Cutheridge.'

'How did you know?'

'My landlady asked old mother Simmeter. Heard she'd been ill, so she went round to see if she could help. She stayed for a chat, and didn't get offered so much as a cup of tea and a biscuit.'

'I think that's fairly typical of the Simmeters.'

'I say, you know I told you about that trouble at the Angel. Do you know what it was about?'

'I could make a guess: Len Simmeter called one of the guards or ticket collectors a black bastard, or some such term.'

'You knew.'

'No, I guessed. It's one of his charming little obsessions. He's careful about giving it rein these days, but he's got a very nasty temper underneath. I thought that'd be what landed him in trouble.'

'Isn't it ghastly? What a rotten little sod.'

'Yes,' said Simon, as if pronouncing a long-pondered judgment. 'I think he's one of the most unappetizing people I've ever met.'

'Oh look—over there. Do you know him?'

Simon peered through the murk at a tall man of thirty or so, standing by the bar.

'I don't think so. Should I?'

'That's Mr Blore. He used to have your room.'

'Really? I assumed he'd moved out of the area. I say, do have another one.'

Rosemary's landlady's cold seemed to have become a matter of lesser importance. She pushed her glass across with a smile. As Simon waited for the landlord to get off his fat beam and condescend to serve, he turned to the tall man and said:

'You don't know me, but I gather I've got your old room.'

'Really?' said Blore, in a manner more pitying than aggrieved. 'Well, rather you than me. I served my sentence.'

'I feel rather guilty about it. I had the impression that Len Simmeter might have hurried you out.'

'He turned me out. I knew he must have someone else lined up. It was the best thing that could have happened to me: I've got two good rooms now for the same rent. Len had been at daggers drawn with me since he saw my Labour Party poster. I think I only stayed on for devilment, to annoy him. I presume the object of the exercise was to up the rent still further?'

'I suspect so,' said Simon. 'I pay four pounds ten.'

Blore whistled.

'But that's ludicrous. It's daylight robbery. And probably

illegal to boot. I bet he's operating with two receipt books or something. You should dob him in.'

'Oh no,' said Simon. 'I shan't be dobbing him in for that.'

'Well, someone ought to. You may have got yourself in with that gorgeous little tottie from next door, but you shouldn't stay a moment longer than you need.'

'The Simmeters have a fatal fascination, as you found.'

'They have nothing of the kind. Len Simmeter's not only a capitalist swine, he's a fascist capitalist swine. Did you know that?'

'Yes,' said Simon. 'That's one of the things I've found out.'

Then Simon carried the glasses back to the table, and for the rest of the evening he forgot about the Simmeters. As he walked home with Rosemary he promised to take her round the Zoo.

'I must remember I've got to take Miss Cosgrove round too. She has the other room on the second floor.'

'Oh well, we can organize it so you take us both together.'

'No,' said Simon. 'I think I'll take you round on your own.'

The question of moving from the Simmeters' came up again by chance next day at the Zoo. He and a senior colleague were standing observing a puma that was taking badly to captivity. While they were watching the moping beast, his companion turned to him and said:

'Done anything about getting a flat nearer here yet?'

'No, not yet.'

'Because I think the Boss is getting a bit worried. He's wondering if you're thinking of moving on, and he doesn't want to lose you.'

'That's nice of him, but it's nothing like that. It's just—well, laziness I suppose. I'll start looking for something more convenient as soon as summer's over.'

And suddenly Simon realized that he was telling the truth. He was going to be moving out from the Simmeters' soon.

That quest to find out about his origins had suddenly begun
to lose the fine edge of urgency. He no longer had any need
to 'find a father'. He had found him, and would quite
happily unfind him at any time. The moment he compared
Len Simmeter with Tom Cutheridge back in Yeasdon, his
heart yearned back to the slow, warm old man. The nature
of his quest seemed to be changing, from an emotional one
to a purely intellectual one: it was less a question of 'who
am I?' and more one of finding out what had happened to
his mother, and how he had turned up on that platform in
Paddington. Any emotion, any urgency, was connected with
his mother: he wanted to know what exactly had happened
on the night she died.

The next evening he called in at the Paddington Reference
Library on his way home from work. What he was interested
in now was Mary Simmeter's death. It should be easy
enough to determine the date. He called for the volume of
the *Recorder* for 1941. It was much lighter than the others he
had handled: newsprint was scarce, though news itself there
was in an abundance that even the 'thirties had not known.
He turned to the week he had arrived in Yeasdon. Got it in
one.

From the yellow pages of the emaciated issue of the paper
there came a dim echo of the horrors of that week. It was
one of the worst weeks of the blitz, and in that May London
was strafed over and over again. On the front page, and
again on the inside ones, there were pictures of blazing
buildings, of houses and public buildings reduced to rubble.
On page five, closely squeezed up together, as if in a journal-
istic paupers' grave, there was a list of casualties. Mary
Simmeter was killed—no precise date was given, but the
issue of the paper was dated May 12th—by the bomb
that had demolished 24 Fisher Street. Simon frowned. The
address meant nothing to him. He drew a finger down the
huddled list of names: finally he came to Simon and Eve
Rosebourne, and their daugher Helen, aged three, all killed
at 24, Fisher Street. So the presumption was that Mary had

been out visiting, or perhaps on an errand of mercy, when she was killed.

The rest of the evening Simon spent in the Colonel Monk. Teddy Simmeter did not come in, but Rosie Short did. They talked, exchanged confidences, got very close. At one point in the evening Rosie said:

'You've got a reason for coming here, haven't you? You weren't just joking?'

'No, I wasn't joking.'

'I bet it's something to do with those rotten Simmeters.'

'Yes, in a way it has.'

'No "in a way" at all. It has. Are you going to tell me?'

Simon paused and thought.

'Yes, I expect some day I will. Not now.'

'You're not one of those shut-in, secretive people, are you?'

He put his arm round her.

'No. I promise you I'm not that.'

It was Friday night when Teddy finally came in. There were rather more customers in the bar than usual, and people coming in and out for bottles the whole time, but Simon recognized Teddy at once. In spite of the twenty-odd years that had passed, there was still something of that young boy in RAF rig he had glimpsed in the Simmeters' sitting-room. Not that time had dealt lightly with him. Then he had been a fresh-faced, shy, not unhandsome young pilot, taking on the planes, presumably, that were inflicting such punishment on London night after night at the time of Mary Simmeter's death. Now he was a pudgy businessman, or more accurately a fat one. He was one of those men who made you wonder about the logistics of trousers; his face was red and veined, under an increasingly sparse head of hair, and he had a double chin round and succulent as turkey breast. But there was about him an air of invincible jollity, of honest roguery, of taking life as it came that was perhaps a relic of his Battle of Britain days. The Simmeter strain only came out in his tendency to corpulence, but whereas his mother's bulk, even in her decline, seemed ponderous, overbearing, threatening, in him the bulk had been transformed—'laundered', one might say, as dubious money is in the States—into something rubicund, endearing, almost Pickwickian. And those small, mean, Simmeter eyes has passed him by altogether.

Simon decided on a direct approach. He was an open soul by nature, and in any case too many devious approaches led to people comparing notes and finding discrepancies. Drinking down the quarter of a pint that remained in his glass, he marched over to the bar and stood by Teddy.

'You must be Teddy Simmeter,' he said. 'I recognize you from your photograph.'

'Such is fame,' said Teddy, a genial smile on his ruddy face. 'Now all I need to hear is that you're from the CID's 'Wanted Persons' department. No, wait!' He banged his fist against his forehead. 'I know who you are. You're the young chap from upstairs.'

'That's right.'

'I've just been hearing about you. Connie was full of you, and even the old Ma said you were a well-spoken young man.'

'That was nice of her.'

'Wrung from her, of course. It's not in Ma to approve a member of the younger generation. They've been going further and further to the bad since the old Queen died, if you believe Ma. I shouldn't laugh at her, poor old thing. She's looking a bit like the old Queen in her last days herself.'

'Is she still poorly?'

'Looks like a wreck of her old self. 'Course, you won't have seen her in her prime: the true British battle-axe, honed to a vicious cutting edge.' He downed his first pint, and pushed his glass across the bar for another. 'But when they get to that age, you forgive all, that's what I say. What she wants is cheering up. Not that it's easy. I feel like Max

Miller in a Wednesday matinée at the Wimbledon Empire. Still, it's better than fighting with her, like Len.'

'I gathered from Len that she didn't want to hand over the reins.'

'Nor she does. But he needn't rub in her weakness in the way he does. She's always held the purse-strings, Ma. Len's always handed over his weekly wage, like a good little boy. Then she starts getting forgetful, and Len starts bit by bit to get control. Nastiness and bitterness all the way, and all over a few quid. What Len really enjoys is showing her who's boss now.'

Teddy took out his wallet.

'I'm going to take a bottle of Scotch back. Len's too mean to buy her anything—and of course the stubborn old body says she doesn't want it, and it goes against her religion. Sign of weakness, that's what alcohol is, as she's told me many a time in the past. Which doesn't mean she's not sitting at home now, hoping I bring a bottle back with me.'

'What do you do?'

'TV rentals and repairs. We're the straightest firm this side of Guildford—though mind you' (he winked) 'the competition's not too hot. That's another sign of weakness, TV. "I won't have a television receiver in the house," she always used to say when I offered her one. In the end I just brought one round and left it. She needs something to cheer her up. She's never been what you'd call a lively spirit herself, and Len's got all the brightness and vivacity of a twenty-five-watt bulb. They just sit around spreading pools of gloom. At least the telly gives her something to tut-tut over.'

'And there's your sister. She seems a bit different.'

'Connie's not going to waste any effort on Ma. Don't get me wrong. Connie's OK. At least she's got a bit of fun in her. But there's too much water's gone under that bridge, too many things in her past that Ma never tires of reminding her of, for her to care much whether Ma is comfortable or not. She just uses the place as a hotel—and there's no love lost between her and the proprietors.' He took a hefty swig at his second pint, and ordered a bottle of whisky. 'No, it's a dismal house and no mistake. My wife refuses to come round, ever since Ma called her a painted strumpet. I don't try to force her: it was pitching it rather high, just for a bit of Boots lipstick. The kids stopped coming years ago. I come round when I start feeling guilty. I can take Ma and Connie, but Len gives me the gripes. He was bad when he was under her thumb, but he's worse now that he's wriggling out from under. Ah well! Back to the Happy Haven!'

He downed the last of his beer, took up the whisky in his pudgy hand, and began making for the door.

'I'll walk along with you,' said Simon. 'Time I was getting back.'

'Right you are. Home to Bleak House, Glum Terrace together. They'll have been counting the minutes I've been gone. The old Ma will say: "You'll never succeed in business if you drink all the profits." And when I produce the whisky it'll be: "Wasting your money like that. Don't pretend *I* want it." And when he sees the bottle Len's piggy little eyes will gleam. Have you got a family?'

'Yes, I have,' said Simon. 'A very nice one.'

'Count yourself lucky. I sometimes wonder how I ever came through without being all knotted up inside, like Len. I used to tell my sister-in-law—Len's wife, poor soul—that she ought to get away with her little boy before they got twisted too. But she never managed it. Me—I was lucky. You could say the war was lucky for me, just as it was unlucky for her. I was in it from the start, almost. Got away, among normal people, and stayed away. Well, here we are—'

'I'll say goodnight,' said Simon.

'Here, look: why don't you come down and have a nip of this with us? Relieve the atmosphere, like. Won't be any fun, I warn you, but you'd be very welcome.'

'Thanks,' said Simon. 'I'd like that.'

'Right. Here we go. Childe Whatsit and friend to the dark tower came. Mind the steps.'

CHAPTER 12

The scene in the Simmeter sitting-room was a long way short of festive. Teddy had let himself in with his own key, and when he appeared at the door from the hallway they were all three looking up at him expectantly—rather as the inhabitants of an old people's home might look up at an amateur conjuror with an expression that said: 'Entertain us. We challenge you to entertain us.' Mother was sitting idly in a chair; Connie, in a smart dress of light blue, had *Woman in the Home* on her lap; and Len was at the table, stewing over a grubby little notebook. Mother sniffed, Connie smiled a lazy smile of welcome, and when he saw Simon behind Teddy Len got up, stretched his mouth into a smile, and began rubbing his hands. It was Mother that Teddy directed his attentions to, but she looked so drawn and tired, bore such signs of a long struggle against human weakness, that it looked to Simon as if he would have an uphill struggle.

'I've brought you a bottle, and I've brought you a guest,' said Teddy heartily, as if he were only augmenting an atmosphere already cheery. 'What more could you want?'

'You shouldn't have,' said his mother, and she seemed to intend the remark to apply to both of his gifts. 'You spend money like water. You know I never brought you up to have drink in the house. It's money wasted: don't pretend *I* want it.'

'Come on, Mother—just a little nip. It'll warm you up.'

He turned towards her inquiringly. Simon had already noticed the dull gleam in Len's eye—not the gleam of an alcoholic, but the gleam of a person who likes getting something—anything—for nothing.

'Well, I won't say no,' Len said.

'That's the ticket,' said Teddy, with his imperturbable jollity. 'Hear that, Ma? I'll just pour you a little nip. Warm the cockles of your old heart—that's what I bought it for.

And I brought along young Simon here to toast your health.'

'Hmmm.'

'Oh, pour one, for Christ's sake,' said Connie, under her breath. 'You know damn well she always drinks it.' Aloud she asked, hostessly: 'And how will you have it, Mr Cutheridge?'

'Simon. With a little water, if I may.'

'With a little water,' said Connie to Teddy, making no effort to get up. 'Neat for me, and a bit of warm water in Mother's.'

Teddy bustled off to the kitchen, and there was a clink of glasses on a tray, and the sound of running water.

'Well,' said Len, who had been lurking angularly in the shadows. 'This is a real little party. We should have done this before. Fancy you running into Teddy.'

'Oh, I was in the Colonel Monk,' said Simon casually. 'I often go.'

'Do you now? Thought you hadn't been upstairs so much recently. Well, I'm glad you did run into him. I'd been meaning to ask you down for a long time.'

'*I'd* hoped to ask you down for a meal,' said Connie, trying on him a practised smile such as she might use on a customer who bore the marks of gentry-hood. 'It's the least we can do.' For Simon's ears only she added, *sotto voce*, 'Considering the rent you pay.'

'Here we are, then. Here we are,' said Teddy, bustling back into the room with his Cheeryble good humour. Imperviousness to atmosphere must, Simon decided, be his way of dealing with the Simmeter ill-humour and mean-mindedness. 'Here's your neat one, Connie. Bit of warm water for Ma. Water for Simon, soda for me and Len. Right you are, everyone. Down the hatch and don't give up hope. Be happy while you're living, for you're a long time dead.'

They drank.

'In the circumstances, Teddy,' said Connie, honey-sweet of voice, 'I think "Bottoms Up" might have been a happier toast.'

'Why?' said Teddy. 'What did I say?'

'Well, we may have time to enjoy ourselves while we're living, but in the nature of things Ma won't have that long, will she?'

'Connie!' said Teddy, shocked out of his good humour.

'They want me dead,' announced the old woman bitterly, the voice heavy with regret at her own enfeeblement, regrets for the victories she had won over her children in the past. 'Any excuse to rub it in they take. They're sitting around waiting for me to die!'

'Lay off it, Ma,' said Len, sharply. 'Tonight of all nights. Can't you see we've got a visitor?'

'*I* didn't invite him. I'm just making it clear to Teddy what I have to put up with. These two want me dead, and I'm not going fast enough for them.'

'Well, you're going a lot too fast for me, Ma,' said Teddy, sounding more than a touch desperate. 'You want a bit of feeding up—not to mention brightening up. You don't look a patch on when I was here last.'

'Is it surprising, with this lot rubbing their hands at every little sign of weakness?' The old woman's voice took on the tones of a particularly doleful contralto. 'They want me gone so they can get their hands on the house and money. They're scared to death I'll change the will and leave it all to you.'

'You silly old biddy,' snapped Len, 'you're making this up. Nothing of the kind's ever been said.'

She turned on him with a formidable, effortful gathering of strength.

'Don't you give me barefaced lies in my own house. It's been said often enough. And when it hasn't been said it's been thought. You sit there, the pair of you, thinking who's going to get what when I'm gone.'

'Now *that's* your imagination, Ma,' said Teddy.

'*I've* got better things to think about, I know that,' said Connie coolly. 'I couldn't speak for Len.'

Len swung round.

'We can do without your insinuations. Showing us up before guests.' He turned back, and toned down his manner to a filial concern. 'It's a real nightmare, you going on like this, Ma. After all the years I've been with you, looking after you. None of the others have done the same, that you must admit, Ma.'

'It wasn't done for love,' said Mrs Simmeter dismissively.

'By-y-y Christ!' exploded Len, savage again. Simon could see he would like to have added: 'How could it have been?'

'Anyway, Ma, that property business was settled years ago,' said Teddy, trying against the odds to re-establish a comfortable tone. 'Len gets the house, Connie gets the bit of money in the bank, I get a little something to remember you by. That's how I wanted it. I'm not complaining, and if I'm not, who is? I'm the one who left the nest—and I've done very nicely for myself on the whole.'

'You won't go on doing if you throw your money around on drink the way you do,' observed his mother sourly.

'Stow it, Ma. Drink it down and warm yourself up.'

'I think this discussion could well be brought to a close,' said Connie, stretching herself comfortably in her chair. 'Teddy, Mr Cutheridge's glass is empty. Get him another one, do.' And as Teddy bustled up, she handed him her own glass, as if he were the bar waiter. 'You must wonder at us, Simon, really you must. Do all families go on like this, or is it just us?'

'In our family there's nothing much to leave,' said Simon. 'We live in a tied cottage, and there's little or nothing put away. Quite apart from the fact that I'm an only child.'

'There you are, you see. Very sensible, your parents. No problem at all if there's only the one.'

'Unless you lose him,' said Len, bitterly. He came to sit by Simon on the sofa. 'My David was an only son. Perhaps we should have had more. I'd have felt the loss less keenly. But it wasn't to be.' He gazed down at the carpet, seeming genuinely to be sunk in thought. 'If only he'd lived ... Things would have been different ... Now there's only Teddy's two, and we hardly know them.'

'You can always leave the ancestral home to the British Union,' said Connie, waspishly breaking in on his thoughts. 'I'm sure they could find a good use for it. As for me, if I survive Ma—which I'm *not* banking on, because you're tough as old boots, Ma, you know you are—if I get that little nest-egg I'm going to use it to have a good time. A bit of moderate whoopee, that's what I'm going to give myself.' She giggled spitefully. 'So don't worry your heads as to who's going to get it after me. There'll be no pickings when I pop off!'

'I wasn't, Connie, I wasn't,' said Teddy with a sigh, returning with the refreshed glasses.

'Oh, I wasn't referring to you, Teddy. You know that. You've always been good to me, and I'm grateful. If I had anything to leave it'd be you I'd give it to, but somehow I don't think there will be. I think I'll branch out. I can't see myself stopping here in this dump with just Len. I could get myself a nice little service flat . . . meals sent up . . . It might just run to that. I have a gentleman friend in property who could advise me. He says they're not expensive, when you consider the convenience of it.'

Suddenly the voice of Mrs Simmeter rang out in a wail.

'You're all sitting round here waiting for me to die!'

'Whatever gives you that idea, Ma?' asked Connie sweetly.

'Teddy—it's like this every night of my life now. They're trying to worry me into the grave. If only you'd stayed. You're not like them. If only you'd stayed—not joined up, not married that painted creature.'

'Now then, Ma: I'm not staying if you start in on that.'

'All right, I won't, Teddy. But you can't deny that we were in trouble, and you got out.'

'Children do, Ma. This isn't India or somewhere. Kids leave the family home. I wasn't to know you'd be in trouble. I went because there was a war on.'

'Teddy fought for his country,' said Connie meaningfully.

'Ah well—' said his mother.

'*Ah well*, you'd rather I hadn't. I know that by now, Ma. We had that out often enough, then and since. You'd rather I'd fought for the other lot, if the truth be known. But you and Len never succeeded with me there—not with me, nor with Connie.'

'Here, hold on, Teddy,' said Len, whose characteristic caution seemed to be reasserting itself. 'We've got guests.'

'All right. Enough said. But don't think I don't remember all the mullarkey we had about it at the time. With me only eighteen, and you two going on at me day and night. It was no fun, living at home those last eighteen months before I joined up, with only Mary I could talk to about it. She was the only one in the family with a grain of human feeling. And you'd have been a damn sight worse, Len, if you hadn't been shit-scared of being investigated—taken in and interned.'

'I told you, Teddy, belt up about that.' Len's face had become a deep pink, in perturbation.

'That's you all over, Len,' said Connie, still aggravatingly relaxed and comfortable in her chair. 'All big aggressive talk, like you were about to lead the troops into battle and become Gauleiter of London. Then at the first sign of anyone fighting back, you go nose first down your burrow. One minute you're screaming revolution, the next you're diving for cover.'

'Shut your mouth, Connie. A lot you know about it.'

'I know plenty. I was back home by then, remember. I remember the way you made us scuttle out of Paddington, half way across London, just because when the chips were down you hadn't the nerve to face things. I remember plenty about you and your wartime doings . . . ' She took a swig from her glass. 'And don't you forget it.'

Len shot her a glance, half cowed. But then his sense of grievance got the better of him.

'I didn't notice you taking up your country's struggle,' he said, his mouth twisted satirically. 'Spent most of the war on your back, as far as I remember. As you'd spent the peace.'

To Simon's surprise, Connie merely giggled. The whisky was beginning to have an effect.

'Golly, Len, you must sound prehistoric to Simon here. Positively out of the ark. As if I ought to be ashamed of giving a bit of warmth and comfort to a few boys who'd be out on a bombing raid in a few hours' time, or on the Normandy beaches. Well, I can tell you, I'm not ashamed at all.'

'My own daughter,' moaned Mrs Simmeter.

'Shame was never exactly your line,' sneered Len.

'It never needed to be. As to spending most of the war on my back, that's just your sex-ridden little mind. I'd rather take pleasure from that, anyway, than from what you got your kicks from. You got more pleasure from roughing your wife up, so far as I could see, than from the other thing.'

'Don't give me that!' roared Len.

'Poor wet little sap, to take it from you.'

'You hold your tongue. We was happy—deliriously happy. Till you came back home, to put a spoke in the wheel.'

'Oh, very happy, provided she did every blind thing you told her to, and she agreed with every word you said.'

'Mary knew what her duties were, and she did them. That's something you'd never understand. She wasn't one of your rackety modern women, to flop into bed with the first man who asked her.'

'Too bloody scared, you saw to that,' said Connie, her good humour unabated. She sat at ease in the chair, smiling cat-like over her whisky, obviously intent on mischief. 'You were always first-rate at terrorizing the weak and sickly. And of course Mum did her bit as well, as per usual. If Mary hadn't been under the thumb of the pair of you, she might have had a bit of life of her own. If I'd been her, I'd have fancied Teddy here a damned sight more than I would you. And Teddy was around—nice and available.'

'Cut it out, Connie,' said Teddy, his cheerfulness now entirely vanished, and seeming to be genuinely outraged.

'It's sick, that sort of talk. I was only in my teens, and Mary was well over thirty. There wasn't anything like that, and you know it.'

'I didn't say she *did*, did I?'

'It was quite different. I appreciated her.' Teddy's eyes had glazed over, and for a few moments Simon caught a touching glimpse of the young, uncertain teenager who lay buried in the flesh of the jolly proprietor of a slightly dubious business. 'She was very understanding. Always. I think she suffered herself, so she had sympathy. I was young —younger than my years, because I'd always been leant on, kept under. And those two had me all knotted up . . . they near drove me to a breakdown. And she . . . just let me talk to her. Talk it through. I told her everything, how I wanted to join up . . . to get away . . . to do something for my country. It sounds old-fashioned now, and perhaps that was partly imagination. What I really wanted was to get out. It's no use looking like that, Ma, because that's how it was. It was my only chance of growing up. And she listened to me . . . '

'You ought to be ashamed of making my wife listen to drivel like that,' said Len. 'If she'd had any sense she would have sent you away with a flea in your ear.'

'But she didn't. She understood. She knew how it was from . . . from her own situation. But she had the little boy, little David, and she couldn't break out.'

'She never wanted to break out!' spluttered Len.

'Well, have it your own way, Len. Perhaps you're right. Certainly she never said as much, because that wasn't her way. The main thing was I felt she sympathized. She let me talk, encouraged me to do what I wanted to do. It wasn't that she wanted me to join up. She thought I was too young. But she saw I had to get away, and she couldn't see any other way. In the end I was one of the first in.'

'I don't see the problem,' drawled Connie. 'After all, I'd got away. And it was more difficult for a girl.'

'You got away. But you'd had to come back. I saw the

sort of thing that could happen. I saw I not only had to make a break: I had to make a permanent break. Mary agreed it would have to be for good.'

'I'm damned sure she never said anything of the kind,' said Len. 'She was much too loyal.'

'But she did. She saw the problem. We'd been kept so close, all of us (her too, in a different way, because her father was a tartar). We hardly knew the world, hardly knew how to make a decision for ourselves. So I knew it had to be a proper break, and I had to talk about it before I made it.'

'Well, you made it,' said Mrs Simmeter grimly. 'You made your bed, and you must lie on it. You were right down disloyal, that's the long and the short of it.' But the iron lines of her face crumpled. 'Oh, if only you hadn't! You wouldn't have been to me like these two have been!'

'I don't know, Ma. If you'd kept me under, I'd probably have turned out pretty much like Len. Well—not quite. I don't think I'd ever have been quite like Len. But I would have been cowed and bitter . . . The only one who wasn't bitter was Mary.'

'I think we've had enough of Mary—' began Len.

'I saw how things were going after Connie came back.'

'Don't blame *me*.'

'I don't, Connie, but there it was. As long as she'd do exactly what Len told her and not question his judgment, things jogged along pretty evenly. And they'd had the baby, to keep them together. But when Connie came back . . .'

'Don't you think,' said Len, standing over Teddy and talking loudly, attempting to use the authority of the male of the house, 'that we've treated Mr Cutheridge to quite enough of the family's business?'

'I could see then,' said Teddy, ignoring him, 'that things weren't going to jog along as they had been doing. Not that things had been good, but they'd been—well—tolerable for all concerned. Oh, I don't blame you, Connie, but you shouldn't have come back, not in the circumstances. And when Len started—'

'I told you, Teddy, I'm not having any more of this before strangers,' bellowed Len, his face now purple with suppressed rage.

'Len's right,' said his mother, painfully hauling herself to her feet. 'I've never known you like this, Teddy. We've never been ones to broadcast our business to all and sundry. We've kept ourselves to ourselves.'

'Oh yes, we've done that,' said Teddy, pulling himself out of his reverie. 'The Simmeter family motto.'

'I'm off to my bed,' said Mrs Simmeter, moving herself slowly and heavily towards the kitchen. 'I'm disappointed in you, Teddy, going on like that. I never imagined you'd talk of your own mother like that, in front of outsiders. It's the drink, and you can't say I haven't warned you against *that*.'

'I must be going,' said Simon hurriedly, standing up and giving Len his glass. 'It's been very pleasant . . . '

Connie burst out laughing.

'A real laugh-a-minute party!'

Teddy suddenly seemed to come completely back to the present, and was terribly ashamed at what he'd let Simon in for. He took his glass back from Len.

'No you don't, young man. You're going to have one for the road, now Ma's off. We'll show you we're not quite the miseries we must have seemed. If you're an only child you won't really understand about families. We have a lot to get off our chests in a short time, now and again. You'll have another, won't you, Connie? And I know Len won't say no . . .'

From the kitchen came the sound of Mrs Simmeter collecting together milk bottles. Teddy was walking round the sitting-room, bottle in hand, pouring generous measures.

'Come on: the night is young. Len—would you go and get a jug of water? And see if there's any soda left. I told Cyn I wouldn't be back till half past eleven. We'll all have a nightcap, and then I'll be off.'

Standing somewhat awkwardly, holding his glass and trying to pretend that the evening still held some potential for festiveness, Simon was facing the door into the hall, and could see straight through to the kitchen. Len was by the sink, filling a jug. Then he turned the tap off, and collected a bottle from the kitchen table. Simon, smiling forcedly (and fatuously, he felt) as Teddy tried to make conversation, heard the milk bottles clink; and then suddenly there came a grunt, a scream, and a heavy thud.

'Oh!' he heard the voice of Mrs Simmeter cry out, in a compound of outrage and pain. 'Oh God! Come and help me! Len! Teddy! Oh God—help me!'

Simon and Teddy put down their glasses and raced into the kitchen. Connie remained seated in her chair. The back door was open, and a light shone on three stone steps, wet with rain. Len was standing by the table looking towards the doorway, through which could be seen a shapeless, floundering bundle of flesh and clothes at the bottom of the steps. As they ran towards the back door, Len turned on them a haggard, terrified face, and caught Simon by the arm.

'I wasn't anywhere near her!' he shouted, bringing his face up close to Simon's. 'Bear witness that I was nowhere near her!'

CHAPTER 13

It was Simon, finally, who called the ambulance. He and Teddy had hauled Mrs Simmeter up the back steps, her bulk, and the pain she was in, adding to their difficulties. Their task was not lightened by Len, who flapped around them in a state of panic which he seemed unable to bring under control. The struggle was watched by Connie, who stood in the kitchen doorway, smoking, and looking on with interest but without concern.

It was obvious as soon as they got the old lady on to a kitchen chair that this was no simple case of a sprained ankle. Mrs Simmeter was doubtless in many ways an unendearing character, but she was certainly not one to exaggerate her woes to gain public sympathy. When Simon said he'd ring for an ambulance Teddy nodded from a position down on his knees removing his mother's shoes. Len looked frightened and seemed about to protest, as if the proposal went against all his instincts for concealing family matters within the confines of the burrow. But finally he too nodded. Simon, in any case, had barely waited for his consent before he ran off to the phone in the hall.

The ambulance came very quickly indeed. When the siren was heard in Miswell Terrace the shapeless mass of woman huddled on the chair was still emitting sharp cries of pain from time to time, and breathing very hard. Her two sons were fussing round her ineffectually, in the manner of men of their generation in times of domestic crisis, but Connie was still standing by the door, a new cigarette between her fingers, and when the doorbell rang she made no attempt to go and answer it. Simon did that too, and ushered through to the kitchen the two men with the stretcher. They loaded Mrs Simmeter on to it with a brisk but tender efficiency which quietened her cries more effectively than all her sons' ministrations had done. Connie watched them from the doorway, as if she were the inadvertent witness to a street accident, and was memorizing details for the police.

'Anyone coming with her?' asked the chief ambulance man.

'Yes, we'll all come,' said Teddy.

'Oh, come *on*, Teddy,' protested his sister. 'I've had a long day. I'm tired. What the hell point is there in all of us going?'

'She might need something—some woman's thing—something you could help with.'

'What in heaven's name are nurses for?'

'*Connie*,' said her brother. 'You ought to come. Please. For me.'

'For crying out loud,' breathed Connie. But she marched into the living-room, fetched her handbag, and took her coat off a peg in the little hallway.

The ambulance men had problems with the stretcher in the meagre dimensions of the house. Just turning from the kitchen into the hall was dicey, and the two steps that divided the Simmeter living quarters from the hall that was common to all the residents proved tricky to negotiate. Finally they got her through the front door and out into the road. There a little knot of casual gazers, dawdling home after closing time, had been attracted by the siren. Len glared at them angrily. 'Push off, can't you?' he shouted, but they stared stonily back. The ambulance men manoeuvred the ungainly mass into the capacious back of the vehicle. Then, still watched by the little group, intent on milking the situation of its limited dramatic potential, Len marched up the steps, fuming. Teddy followed, and finally Connie walked up into the vehicle in an aggressively leisurely fashion, having stubbed out her cigarette on the road with her high-heeled shoe. The ambulance men pushed up the collapsible steps, shut the back, and within seconds the ambulance had driven away.

Simon watched it till it turned the corner. The small knot of people dispersed, to relate the little excitement beerily to wives or loved ones. Simon turned and went back into the house. He shut the front door carefully behind him, and was about to mount the stairs when a thought struck him. He padded over to the door leading to the Simmeters' quarters and tried the handle.

In their haste they had forgotten to lock it.

Simon closed it again, noiselessly, then stood for a moment in thought. It was not that he was in any doubt as to what he was going to do. But the code he had been brought up in, the code of the Cutheridges, was a simple and honourable one, and when he departed from it—as, in the life he led, more complex than the Cutheridges', he found he often had to do—he needed time to contemplate his deviation, set it in a moral perspective. He was still not quite ready to open that door again when he heard a noise from the second floor.

With a strong feeling that he was doing something unworthy of him, he began guiltily to mount the stairs.

'What's been going on down there?' came the voice of Miss Cosgrove, who was looking over the banisters.

'Old Mrs Simmeter. She fell down the back steps,' called Simon, continuing up.

'Hmmm. Beginning of the end, I shouldn't wonder. She's been looking ghastly recently.'

Turning into the second flight, Simon was surprised to see that Miss Cosgrove was in an outdoor coat and carrying a suitcase.

'I'm off on holiday. I think I told you about it—Florence. These package tours always have flights at such dreadful times. *And* it's my first experience of flying. I have to keep telling myself how much extra time I'll have there. I don't mind telling you, I'll be glad when we land at Pisa.'

'I'll take your case.'

'That is kind. These stairs are so poky. I'm going to hail a cab at the corner, then get the bus from Victoria. I heard cries. Was the old lady in much pain?'

'Yes—great pain, or so it seemed. Something more than just a sprain, anyway.'

'I'll say this for her: she's not one to make a fuss needlessly. Did Len and Connie go with her?'

'Yes—and Teddy. He was round on a visit. He'd invited me in, so I was there. Connie was pretty reluctant to go.'

'She would be. No love lost there: some kind of grudge that goes back a long way, I'd guess. Not to mention that she's a lazy cow at the best of times, pardon my language. Len will be pleased if his mother goes, that's for sure. Len likes to rule the roost—*any* roost—and he'll never get control as long as the old lady's alive. Not to mention the money. The way they live, they could well have put a fair bit away over the years, in their hole and corner manner.'

'I gather Connie gets the money.'

'You *have* learnt a lot about them.'

'They've been baring their souls down there tonight.'

'Ugh. How very unpleasant. I shouldn't care for that at

all. No, don't come any further. Now you've got it downstair
I can carry it quite easily.'

'Have a good holiday. I'll take you around the Zoo wher
you come back.'

'I'm looking forward to it.'

'Ring me at the Zoo if I'm not here when you come back.

In the dim light Miss Cosgrove threw him a significan
glance.

'I *thought* you wouldn't be here for long. No reason why
you should be, either. I hope you find somewhere really
nice. Goodbye for now.'

Then, as she made her way towards the cars and lights
of the main road, Simon shut the front door and turned
back into the hall.

This time he did not hesitate. His very feelings of guil
committed him. It was almost as if he had done it already
He went straight from the front door to the Simmeters' door
and through that into their low, dingy scrap of passageway

They had not only left their quarters unlocked, they had
left them lighted. Len was usually lightning quick with the
switches, so he must have been really disturbed. And Connie
had been the last out. Connie didn't give a damn, and Teddy
had been too concerned about his mother. Simon went
through into the living-room. The first thing he did was try
to recreate the moment of Mrs Simmeter's fall. He stood on
the same spot, in the same attitude, holding an imaginary
glass. He thought hard. He had actually, he remembered
been looking through into the kitchen, had been watching
Len at the time. Len had been fetching a bottle of soda from
the kitchen table. He crossed into the kitchen and stood
where he remembered seeing him stand. It was six feet away
from the back door. Simon went to the door, opened it
turned on the back light, and examined both doorway and
steps for any signs of a booby-trap or trip-wire. There were
none. Only skid marks on the slightly mossy stone steps.

Len, then, had not pushed his mother down the steps
nor caused her to fall by any more sneaky means. There

was not a scintilla of suspicion. Yet Len was obviously unaware that Simon had been watching him at the time, and he was evidently shit-scared that someone was going to accuse him of just that. He had hardly moved from where he was until the others had come into the kitchen. Why was he so panic-stricken? Because it was something he had wanted to do? Something he had mulled over in his mind, but had never summoned up the nerve to carry out?

Or was it because he had once done something very similar? Not to his mother, but to his wife?

Simon slowly went back into the living-room. He walked round it, examining the photos he had seen the first time he had been there, now much more resonant from his greater knowledge: the angular wedding picture, so little expressive of joy or anticipation; the young Teddy—eager, happy, slightly defiant; the mother and son, which he scanned once more in the hope that it would stir sluggish memories. Where had he gone with his mother to have this taken? Some studio in Paddington, no doubt. It was posed against a patently bogus background. He and his mother were clearly responding docilely to some professional's direction . But it had been no red-letter day in his young life: it stirred no residue of memory in any corner of his mind.

Perhaps there were more photographs elsewhere? He rummaged through the drawers of the sideboard: bills, account books, cheap rubber stamps that printed 'Received with thanks', some newspaper clippings on Rent Acts and the rights of landlords and tenants. All of these were the impedimenta of the Simmeters' petty capitalism. In the big cupboard at the bottom were piled parts of a heavy and hideous dinner service, in a design of dark green leaves and claret-coloured flowers. There were heavy cut-glass jugs and bowls, a set of fish-knives and forks, and a large Bible on the shelf above. It was under the Bible that Simon found the photograph album.

It was a heavy, brown volume, with dark brown pages, probably bought in the 'twenties or 'thirties. As he picked it up, Simon felt sure he was going to be disappointed. It was too light—hardly used. The Simmeters were not camera buffs, and he never would have expected them to be. Their secretiveness would see the camera as an invader rather than as a recorder. Only the first ten or fifteen pages of the album were used, and even on them there were places where photographs had been torn out. Why? Which were these? Simon was willing to bet they were records of Len's activities that he had rushed to obliterate as soon as war broke out.

The figures in the snapshots stared at him, mostly unsmiling. A younger Mrs Simmeter, massive and ramrod-straight, caught on the promenade of some resort, and again on a deckchair on a beach. She seemed determined to record for posterity that *she*, at least, had gained no pleasure from that particular jaunt. Mary Simmeter, clad for summer, on another sea-front, smiling—shyly, uncertainly, as if she were trying to do what was expected of her. Len, in decorously capacious swimming trunks, faking carefree pleasure by the waves. Later there were other members of the family: Teddy in the uniform of the Boy Scouts; Mary beside her father (gaunt, patriarchal, a right tartar); the young Connie in a sleeveless floral dress. It was Simon's first glimpse, this last, of what Connie had looked like when young. Her blonde hair was carefully waved around a pretty face—the face made up, the general effect clearly the result of effort and attention. Though the young Teddy in RAF uniform presented an attractive enough figure, Connie was the only Simmeter who could be described as good-looking. She gazed out of the photograph as if she knew it, and was only waiting for an opportunity to use her looks. There was something slyly provocative about her expression: 'I'm going to show you,' she seemed to be saying.

Simon shut the book, vaguely dissatisfied. He looked around the room, wondering where there might be secrets. He opened drawers, pulled down flaps, rummaged. Nothing of interest. Then a thought occurred to him. This room held, for the most part, the present-day life of the Simmeters, their concerns of the moment, such as they were. But what he was after was a quarter of a century old, and the photograph album was the only thing in this room that held memories of so far back. However real the period was beginning to become to him, it was old history to the Simmeters. Might it not be in the dining-room—so far as Simon knew, hardly ever used—that such memories might be put in cold storage? He left the living-room, went down the passage, and turned on the light in the dining-room.

Deep frozen, Simon decided, might be a better expression than cold storage. On that September night, after a mild day, the room had a damp chill, and a stillness that was not peaceful, merely lifeless. Nothing had been done here for years, nothing had happened. Even the petty frustrations and jealousies of the living-room had not penetrated here. The room was dead—impeccably dusted, but dead.

Even the light was dim. Simon peered around in the gloom. The furniture was predictably unattractive: a heavy table, its legs much afflicted with the knobs and goitres that characterized English middle-class furniture of the period; four chairs neatly drawn up to the sides; an ancient piano in a wood the colour of diarrhœa. It looked as if it had not been touched for decades, and Simon could imagine its hollow-sounding tones, hideously out of key. On a small table beside it, a wind-up gramophone, and on a shelf underneath it a pile of 78 r.p.m. records. Simon did not examine them, for fear they included Dame Clara Butt singing *Land of Hope and Glory*.

And that was all, more or less. Except that under the window (whose curtains, Simon had noticed from the road, were perpetually drawn) was one of those little tables about the purpose of which one could only speculate. It was too small to eat off or write on, too tall to serve as an occasional table. It was less bulbous than most of the Simmeters' furniture but (like them) it had no kind of grace. But it did have drawers. It was the only place in this desert of a room where any kind of personal memento might be kept. Simon, nevertheless, went over to it with no sense of expectation.

The contents were a series of envelopes. The top one was marked MY WILL, with the signature Flora Jane Simmeter. Not unexpectedly, it was sealed. Underneath it was PERSONAL DOCUMENTS, with a note saying 'Birth, Marriage, Death'. It too was sealed. But the envelope under that—containing nothing official, or, who knows, being looked at more often—was unsealed. It was labelled MARY'S LETTERS TO ME, with the initials L.S. in the bottom right-hand corner.

Simon, his heart beating, turned the envelope over and took the letters out. There were only three. One was dated late 1930, and seemed to be from the period of their engagement. Mary was with her father at Leamington Spa, staying with an aunt. She agreed with Len that 11.30 on February 22nd was a very suitable time, and said her father would be arranging the details of the reception on his return to London. There were no expressions of affection beyond the 'love, Mary' at the bottom of the page. The second letter, undated, found Mary staying with the same aunt, who seemed to have been in service, and who was now ill. Mary assured Len (who had obviously been nagging at her) that she would *not* overdo things in her condition, said what worrying times these were to bring a new soul into the world, and said she'd be back on Saturday without fail.

It was the last letter in this meagre collection that interested Simon the most. It was written on two sheets of very poor notepaper—the lined sort, made even shabbier-looking by wartime paper restrictions. Yet from it came some faint air of the real woman who had been Mary Simmeter.

27th February 1941   14 Blenheim Ave,
                                            Cattermole,
                                            Sussex

Dear Len,
    I am staying with the Templetons at the above address, it is a nice place and they seem very nice people, but they

are old, is it right to send a little boy to such old people? Davey is so very small he needs people who can play with him and be with him all the time, thats what I think anyway. Mrs T has arthuritus and could not look after his clothes in the way you and I would wish. But if he must come its very quiet here, almost countryside, and I will be happy to have him away from all the bombs and that, its been like Hell these last months, and I know its affected you though I dont want to talk about that. If only I could be with him Len, but you dont want that, and of course it would be hard on you, but youd have your mother. Also the Templetons want £2 per week, could we afford that? It is awful to think I might not be able to visit very often, what with the raids and all the restrictions. I do hope you will think again and let me come with him, at least for a few weeks if not longer. I could even get a job, it would help, and there is a call for domestic servants, so many doing war work. I will try and get the train on Thursday morning, but heaven knows when it will get to Charring Cross, remembering the journey down, it was a nightmare, it took nearly five hours. Give my love and a hug to Davey. Tell mother I will try to get her some nice cakes, also some ham, I know she likes it, food is more plentiful here. My love to Connie and Ted. See you some time on Thursday, God willing.

Your loving wife,
Mary

Simon stood there, the letter in his hand. Then he read it over again. Something—some attenuated shade—came to him of the loving, put-upon, tenacious little woman who had been Len's wife and his own mother. It struggled up through the uncertain orthography, the stiff phraseology of a woman unused to writing letters. But it wasn't just that. This woman was one who had had little experience of putting forward her wishes openly, of expecting to be listened to. She was

making her views clear now only because what she loved
most was threatened. She was summoning up her strength
because her whole world revolved around the child. Make
demands she could not, but what limited fight she could put
up to stay with him she was determined to make. In the
end, Simon feared, she was a woman who would do what
she was told, however heart-wrenching that proved to be,
because doing what she was told had been her lot throughout
life. A good woman, a strong-principled one, but almost
certainly one of life's losers.

'Well!' came the voice of Connie Simmeter from the
door. 'You *are* showing an interest in our affairs, aren't
you?'

CHAPTER 14

Simon stood there in suspended animation, the letter still
clutched in his hand. His mind seemed to be working
furiously, independent of him, ticking over with calculations
in which he himself scarcely seemed involved. The first
conclusion that the process led to was that this was the
beginning of the end. Now things had to come out into
the open. His days at the Simmeters', as he had already
begun to foresee, were numbered. 'This is it,' his brain
said.

'Well, well,' said Connie, her voice more amused than
accusing, 'we have a spy in our midst. It makes a break in
the monotony, come to think about it. But what on earth
could you be interested in? Wills? Why would you bother
with who gets what in the Simmeter family? Mind you, I
did rather wonder when you got friendly with Len. No
one—just no one—gets friendly with Len. Were you hoping
to worm your way into his confidence? His affections—God
help you? Take the place of the son he lost? I can't see why
you'd bother—you with a good job and prospects. It just

loesn't seem worth your while.'

Simon remained fixed to the spot, staring at Connie. She, on the other hand, was leaning relaxedly against the door. Her face was redder than usual, and from her handbag there protruded the neck of a bottle. She had commandeered Teddy's whisky, to sustain her at the hospital.

'Lost your tongue?' Connie resumed. 'I warn you, you haven't got long. Len remembered as they were wheeling her into the Emergency Ward that he hadn't locked up. As our Len was bound to. He sent me back to do it. If I'm not back at the hospital soon he'll imagine I've been raped by burglars or something, and come back to see what's going on. It's only ten minutes away, as perhaps you didn't know. So you'd better give me your story, because, I tell you, Len would be quite capable of calling the police.'

Simon took his decision.

'I'm trying to find out why Len murdered his wife,' he said.

Now the silence in the room was total. Simon's body gradually relaxed its rigidity. It almost felt as if things were out of his hands. There seemed, when the remark sank in, no diminution in Connie's amiability: on the contrary, on consideration she seemed rather to relish the situation. Pursing her mouth in amused contemplation, she walked over to a cabinet, took out two tumblers, and poured a finger of whisky each for Simon and herself. She brought Simon's over, looked at the letter he was holding in his hand, and then sat herself down unceremoniously on one of the dining chairs.

'Good Lord,' she said, still smiling and swilling the whisky round in her glass. 'After all these years.'

Simon looked at her, faintly repelled by her coolness.

'You're not denying she was murdered?'

She waved his words aside with a pudgy hand.

'Wait . . . wait . . . I'm trying to think who you are. Not police, of course. I can't really believe in the file kept open for decades. Quite apart from the fact that there never was

a file. Nobody had any doubts—no serious ones. There were
more than enough other things for them to worry about at
the time. But who could you be? ... I've got it! The
Spurlings! Mary's people.' Simon allowed himself to smile
ambiguously. 'You're a cut above them, in looks and everything else, I'll give you that. I never could abide that
narrow-minded lot—and they certainly didn't approve of
me. After Mary's father died we never had much contact
with them. They never came round to our place. But Mary
visited them, of course—she was the baby of the family
they loved her. Who had children about your age? Most of
the older brothers and sisters had had their families and
done with it by the time Mary was married. So they'd be
older. But there was Enid, wasn't there? The next oldest
sister. That would be it. You'd be—what?—twenty-seven?
Twenty-eight? You must be one of Enid's. Well I never! To
think they had their suspicions, and held on to them all
these years!'

Simon kept his eyes on her, but she did not abate her
high good humour. She sipped from her glass, apparently
with added relish. Simon said again:

'So you don't deny she was murdered?'

'Oh, murder,' said Connie dismissively. 'I'm no friend to
Len, but I wouldn't call it that. And I don't think the law
would either. What's that other word? Manslaughter. I
should have thought that even the police, if they'd ever
been involved, would have called it manslaughter. And, not
wishing to say a good word for Len (which I've had no
cause to do for many years) still, I do understand how it
happened. I was always very fond of Mary, but I do think
there are some women who actually invite violence. The
submissive type, you know.'

She said it complacently, in a way that angered Simon.

'They only invite violence if they come up against someone who's inclined to violence. Like Len.'

'Like Len. Well, that's as maybe. There's a bit of violence
in all of us, isn't there? I know *I* could have slapped her silly

face now and then, when she used to look at me dumbly, trying to tell me what my duty was. The funny thing is, I believe in the first years of their marriage they were reasonably happy. Not unhappy, anyway. I left home soon after they got spliced, and I didn't go back till 'thirty-nine, but from what I saw on visits they jogged along perfectly comfortably. Len was pleasant enough, as long as she did what he told her. But I'd not deny Len's got a lot of violence bottled up there.'

'Which he mostly got rid of in these rallies and demonstrations, I suppose.'

'Oh—you know about all that, do you? What I call Len's comic opera side. Well, I suppose you would, of course. The Spurlings never did approve of that. It was all Church with your family, and the Mosleyites were never what you'd call respectable. Len took up with them soon after the marriage, and I think old man Spurling (your granddad) bitterly regretted arranging the marriage. Len became a lot too notorious locally for his liking. When you go in for that sort of politics you can't be tactful about it, or keep quiet. Len thought he was part of the wave of the future—poor bugger!—and he proclaimed it from the roof-tops every chance he got. Yes, I suppose you could say he got rid of most of his violence that way.'

'Only when war came, that outlet was stopped.'

'You know, I'd never thought of it in that light, but perhaps you're right. Mary copped it because Len couldn't go goose-stepping through the streets of Paddington.'

To Simon, standing over her, the cool-blooded acquiescence of Connie Simmeter in Mary's fate was almost painful. A smile had been playing around her face since she sat down, and it had now expanded into a richly reminiscent, cat-like expression, wreathing her face in what might be mistaken for good humour.

'Watching Len when the war broke out was a real treat. It was the best revenge I could have had. Half the time he'd be rubbing his hands—you know how he does—and I knew he was thinking that within weeks the Germans would be here. Only he never said so, of course. Just hugged to himself his little vision of what he would be then—the glorious position his faith and loyalty would win for him. But then the rest of the time . . . '

'He was scared stiff?' hazarded Simon.

'Right. Because there was the here and now, wasn't there? Len was the sort who'd never be able to decide to have an operation to save himself pain in the future. When he wasn't thinking of the glorious prospect of Gauleiter Simmeter, he was off his head with fear about what the authorities might do to him *before* the liberating Boche arrived. Oh, it was comic! It was rich!'

She giggled, quite unconscious of the effect her relish was having on her audience.

'It sounds really nasty,' said Simon.

'Not to me. I fuelled it. I just liked sitting there watching him. I'd say: "I see the *Mail* says they should round up all the Fascists as well as the aliens." Len would jump half a foot, and say: "That's rich. Rothermere was always one of our best supporters." And I'd say: "That's why he's so keen to make it hot for you, I suppose." '

'What was it he was afraid of?'

'I don't suppose he exactly knew. Some pretty nasty things happened to suspected German sympathizers in the first war. Internment was the immediate fear. They rounded up all sorts—refugees from Hitler, Jews and that, ordinary Germans who'd been here for years, Nazi sympathizers—and they cooped them all up together . . . And sometimes they shipped them off: Canada, Australia, God knows where. One of the boats was sunk. That terrified Len.'

'I believe Len was taken in for questioning.'

'That's right. You *have* done your homework. The authorities were on to all the right-wing groups from quite early in the war. It was just questioning then. Len was taken in, and of course he told them that, like his Leader, he was praying for an English victory; that as soon as the chips were down he was an Englishman before all else; that the Mosleyites were in fact *super*-patriots, and no one could touch them for enthusiasm for the war. That was their line, I believe.'

'But it wasn't true?'

'As far as Len was concerned it was one big laugh. He'd tried to stop Teddy enlisting, as you heard. You'd only got to watch him reading the papers. As soon as the phoney war ended and they started going into Holland, Belgium, Norway, Len used to sit there reading the news, and snuffling to himself with the pleasure of it.'

Simon glanced at his watch. After midnight. Before long Len might come to investigate, and he wanted to hear Connie's version before that, the view of a comparative outsider.

'What happened between Len and Mary?' he asked.

'Well, not much really . . . not anything you could really pin down, not at first . . . It was all a consequence of him getting more and more jittery. They'd take him in for questioning and that'd scare the pants off him for a few weeks. Hardly a peep out of our Len. Then he'd start getting uppitty again. It wasn't so much what he *said*. That was hardly more than "Won't be long now." It was the way he carried on: throwing his weight around in the house, laying down the law about little things, playing the big boss. Even Mother couldn't do anything with him. She was looking forward to Hitler marching down Whitehall as much as Len was, but she didn't like to see her son getting above himself in her house. She was the boss there, and always had been.'

'She was tarred with the same brush, I gather.'

'Politically? Oh yes, it all went back to Ma. I think that what she loved was power, and she never got enough of it. Dad submitted too easily and died too early. People like Mary just lay down in her path and let her drive over them. It was too easy; there was no relish in it. She loved the Nazis because you could *see* the power, see it being exercised. Oh yes, it was Ma behind Len . . . So, as I say, those early

years of the war were all up and down with Len—no sooner
had he decided the Germans would be here in a couple of
weeks than he'd be hauled in for questioning, or the boss of
the Paddington Mosleyites would be interned. That happened early in 1941. I remember Len panicked—scared
bleeding stiff. "I don't think you're the stuff dictators are
made of," I said. "Not even the tinpot kind." He hit me
then—but I kicked him in the groin. He wasn't often violent
towards me, because he knew I'd hit back, and where it'd
hurt.'

'Unlike Mary.'

'Unlike Mary.' The smile of complacent superiority
mantled her face again. 'Silly cow. She had only to let him
have it once and he'd have given over.'

'What went wrong between them?'

'Oh, a lot of things. Sort of combination of circumstances.
She never went along with him politically, of course. She'd
do what he told her—even take little Davey along to meetings if Len really made an issue of it—but there was always
this silent disagreement. She'd say, "I don't meddle with
politics," but Len knew what that meant, and so did Ma.
Then, when the raids started, she wanted to take Davey out
of London, for his own sake. She wanted to go with him. I
don't think it was just the raids. I think she wanted to get
him away from Len. Give Mary her due, she was a good
mother: if you like the doting parent line you had to admit
she was good with the boy.'

'Why wouldn't he let her go? He always says how fond
he was of the boy.'

'Your guess is as good as mine. Thousands were going
into the country every day, and he said he wanted Davey
out of the raids. Because London was hell—for months on
end it was pure hell. If you want my guess as to why he
wouldn't let her go—'

'Yes?'

'It was pure jealousy. He was jealous of her with Davey.
It wasn't that he wanted Mary in Paddington (though he

did need someone there to bully), it was that he didn't want her in Sussex with the boy. You know Len—suspicious as hell. He thought she'd turn Davey against him. Thought that even if she didn't (and she wouldn't have, she wasn't the type at all), she'd become everything to him, and he, Len, nothing. Davey was the apple of his eye; he never could have borne that. So things got worse between them. Mary never put herself up openly in opposition to him, but there was that dumb resistance—all silent, passive, and doubly aggravating. Len got riled! His own wife! Len was always bloody primeval in his attitudes.'

'So there was . . . violence.'

'Now and then. You don't want to hear details, do you? He roughed her up a bit. First the isolated blow—you didn't need more than that with Mary . . . But then he rather got a taste for it . . . '

'Until he murdered her.'

Connie drank down the last of her whisky, and swivelled round in her chair to face the sad-eyed young man who was standing over her.

'That's your word. I never used that word.'

'You suggested manslaughter.'

'Well, I might go along with that. If you listened to Len you'd think it was nothing more than an accident—pure bad luck. That's nonsense, of course, but you know she was a sickly little thing. Didn't your mother ever mention that? One endless series of complications, her pregnancy. I wouldn't mind betting she had a brittle skull. Of course, if the police had known what happened, they would certainly have charged Len with something—especially as they were so interested in him anyway. It would have given them a handle, and the authorities a propaganda point. But I never entirely blamed him, because he never intended more than roughing her up a bit, and I know I'd have found Mary infuriating if I'd been married to her.'

'You take it very lightly,' said Simon bitterly. Connie shrugged.

'Just being honest. Of course, I *pretended* to blame him . . .'

'To get him worked up? Scared out of his wits?'

'It didn't need me for that. He knocked her to the floor, and when she just lay there and didn't move, he started shouting at her. It was the third or fourth time he'd hit her that night, and he thought he might have gone too far. When she went on just lying there, he was absolutely pissing himself.'

'So you moved the body—'

Connie had pricked up her ears. She had heard something from outside the room. Once again that expression of self-hugging delight appeared on her face.

'Ah well—now you can have the pleasure of telling *him* what you think we did next. Len! In here, Len . . . I knew you'd come back. Guess what Simon here's been doing, Len.'

'What?'

'Looking for evidence to convict you of murder.'

Len's face had been haggard when he came in. At Connie's words he flinched as from an expected blow, and his eyes became wild with fear. Connie had got up, and had said her piece rather as if introducing the two men for the first time. Now she sat on the table, jiggling her foot up and down as if in time to some unheard Beatles song, forgetting even to pour herself a drink. Her mouth was curved into a cat-like smile of anticipated pleasure, and she watched Len's every reaction, every symptom of his panic, with the relish of a connoisseur. Len and his mother were not the only members of the family who enjoyed the exercise of power, who fed greedily on the terrified twistings and turnings of the cornered weak.

'Murder?' said Len, his voice suddenly rising to a squeak, after which he swallowed convulsively two or three times. 'What are you talking about? She's not even dead yet.'

'Who isn't?' asked Simon.

'Mother. She's still alive. They say she'll pull through,

with luck. You must be out of your mind to talk of murder. I was over by the table when she fell. Yards away from her.'

'I know you were,' said Simon . He was in command of the room now, with Len stealing covert glances at him and trying not to catch his eye. Please God let me not get enjoyment from this, said Simon to himself. Aloud he went on: 'I could see you by the table when she cried out. You were nowhere near her. I'm not accusing you of murdering your mother.'

'Well, then,' said Len. His sigh of relief was audible. Suddenly he turned on his sister. 'What the hell do you mean by saying he was? You'll be sorry for this, you bitch.'

'What interested me,' said Simon, breaking in on him, 'was what you said *after* your mother fell.'

Len swung back, his panic renewed.

'Why? What did I say?'

'You said: "Bear witness I was nowhere near her." '

'Well, no more I was. You saw me. You can bear witness.'

'I can,' said Simon, still looking straight at him. 'But that wasn't the reaction of an innocent man, was it? Why should you think you needed anyone to bear witness? Innocent of *this*—but guilty of what? You'd been afraid, for years, of being accused of killing somebody. Who was that some-body?'

'That's nonsense! I was just confused.'

Connie smiled with feline solicitude at her writhing brother.

'You shouldn't imagine he just got this idea tonight, Len. Why do you think he's been all palsy-walsy with you? He's been into it, knows about it all. He was just about to tell me, when you came in, how we moved the body.'

'What body?'

'Your wife Mary's,' said Simon. 'Whom you killed.'

'My wife? I loved my wife. I've told you, I worshipped the ground she walked on.'

Simon took a step closer to him, his eyes still fixed on the terror-stricken face. Len cringed back. Simon spoke as if he were reciting a charge.

'Mary, whom you killed. It was early in the war, and you were all het up. You had to hit out at something, and she was there. You couldn't stand opposition, and you knew that in her heart she stood against you. You hit her—then more, then more still. Real beating. You found you liked it. It gave you something you needed—when the fix of meetings and marches and salutes had been taken away. It was the sort of pleasure you might have had a great deal of, if the war had gone the other way. You enjoyed it, and you went too far.'

'I never did. This is fantasy.' Len was hopping in an ecstasy of panic, and then he turned on his sister. 'What have you been telling him?'

'Make up your mind, Leonard, do. Either it's fantasy, or I've been telling him things. As a matter of fact, I haven't told him anything he hadn't already worked out for himself.'

'Then you moved the body,' resumed Simon, his voice rising a tone or two. 'It was May '41, the last big raids of the Battle of Britain. The sort of marks she had on her could easily have been confused with injuries gained when a house was bombed. Especially when the medical services at the time were stretched almost out of existence. I expect one of you went to prospect for the nearest badly bombed house—'

'Ma,' said Connie. 'Ma went.'

'Then you took her to the house in Fisher Street. Where was that? Through the back yard and into the ruins?'

'Further than that,' said Connie feelingly. 'A bloody sight further than that.'

'You shut your lying mouth.'

'I just said that Fisher Street was further away from Farrow Street than Mr Cutheridge implied,' said Connie in a sweetly genteel voice. 'Where could be the harm in that?'

'And you left her there with the other bodies. And when she was found, I suppose you told the authorities she was visiting there. That they were friends of hers.'

'I always said "slight acquaintances",' said Connie, again

looking with relish at her brother to see the effect of her
words on him. 'I thought there might be relatives or friends
to pop up and say the dead couple had never heard of the
Simmeters. Though as it turned out the poor things were
new in the district, and hardly had any family.'

'Shut your mouth, you bitch,' shouted Len, in a vitriolic
burst of self-assertion. 'You'll make him think this crap he's
imagined is the truth.'

'Well, isn't it?' asked Simon. 'What's your version?'

'I don't need a version. It was accepted at the time. Mary
was out visiting. She was visiting a house that was hit by a
bomb. Everyone in the house was killed.'

Suddenly, to Simon's amazement, Connie began to laugh.
It was a laugh that began small, but billowed out, as if she
had been saving up the humour of it for twenty-five years,
having had nobody with whom she could relish the comi-
cality of the thing.

'Oh dear, Simon: it's a good job nobody had the time to
go deeply into the story at the time. Isn't it, Len? Nobody
seemed to find it at all strange that Mary was out visiting
at the Rosebournes', did they? It never occurred to them.
If they'd looked into it further, they'd have realized that she
never could have been.'

'Why not?' asked Simon, and was greeted by a further
billow of laughter.

'It wouldn't have been allowed. Because they weren't
really called Rosebourne, were they, Len? They were called
Rosenbaum. And they were Jewish. Poor refugees from Nazi
Germany. You wouldn't have let Mary nod her head in the
street to them. We'd put Mary in the home of a Jewish
family!'

'You . . . stupid . . . bitch!' said Len, spitting it out slowly,
trying to endow it with the concentrated bitterness of three
decades.

'The funny thing was . . . ' said Connie, her words still
interrupted by gusts of laughter, 'that we heard afterwards
. . . that the man was on the list of the authorities . . . as a

suspicious alien . . . If things hadn't turned out as they did
. . . he and Len might have been interned together!'

And Connie had her last gleeful laugh over the long-past
pains of others, and then subsided somewhat.

'But as it was,' Simon put in quietly, 'you pulled up your
roots and got the hell out of Paddington.'

'That's about it. Len never really felt safe in Paddington
again. About a month after that he took a job at the Angel,
and we bought this house. Made a big loss on the Paddington
house, but Len insisted. The only thing Len values higher
than money is his own skin. Of course, if anyone had wanted
to trace us, they could have. It wouldn't have been difficult.
But Len insisted no one would go to so much bother, and
for once he was right. He was never called in for questioning
after we moved. You just weren't a big enough fish, were
you, Len?'

'Look,' said Len hoarsely, turning on Simon. 'I want an
end to this. What she's been babbling on about is spite,
nothing but spite. Not a grain of truth in it. You don't
imagine, do you, if you go along to the police with a story
like that, that they'll take you seriously and start looking
into it?'

'No,' said Simon, suddenly strangely weary. 'No, I don't.
I don't think I ever envisaged it becoming a matter for the
police.'

'I heard the word "murder" used,' said Len, feebly aggressive.

'Justifiably, from all I've heard tonight. But you're quite
right: even if I wanted to, I could never get the police
interested. And I'm not sure that I'd do it, even if I could.
I just wanted to know. I'll be getting out of here tomorrow.'

'And why,' demanded Len, his body now held more
confidently, expressing, indeed, an almost cocky confidence
now that he seemed safe, 'should you "want to know" may
I ask?'

'I'm sure he's a Spurling,' announced Connie, with obvious self-congratulation at her own perceptiveness. 'I'd put

my money on one of Enid's. She was one of those dull, plodding women, Enid was, who'd go worrying away at a thing, year in, year out. And she was very fond of Mary. She had a son a year or two older than your David, but I can't remember his name. They never liked us, Len.'

'So you're one of the Spurlings, are you? By Chrr-ist, that was a dull family if you like! I don't congratulate you on your parentage, young man. Pillars of the Baptist Church—that's what you lot are, or were. The Church deserved you, and you deserved the Church, if you ask my opinion. Well, I'll tell you what I'm going to do: in the morning I'm going to send you packing.'

'You won't need to.' Simon still seemed possessed by this great weariness, and he made no attempt to reassert dominance over Len. 'I've found out most of what I was looking for. That you were a bully inside the house as well as out of it. That you mistreated your wife, and when eventually you killed her, you covered up the killing with the help of your family. I think the fear you've lived with since has been some sort of punishment. I hope so. If I've added to it I'm glad. I'd like to think you suffered something for what you did.' He paused. 'There were some other things I'd like to have found out. I'd like to know what happened to your son.'

At his mere mention of the word, there sounded through the room an animal-like cry, a howl of anguish.

'My son!' cried Len. 'You talk about punishment, and then about my son!'

His face was crumpling, as it had in the pub, and he suddenly sank into a chair.

'Oh Gawd,' said Connie, with unshakable calm. 'Don't start him off about his son.'

'You talk about punishment,' howled Len again, his shoulders heaving up and down. 'That was my punishment. If anyone had said, "What's the worst thing that could happen to you?" I'd have said, "To have Davey killed in a raid." And that's what they did to me. Some Luftwaffe pilot on his way home, just getting rid of his surplus stuff. On my David. If you want me punished, then you're too late. That was it. Talk about suffering—a boy like you doesn't know what suffering is. I wish I'd died the day I heard.'

There was something so anguished, so intense, so drained about the man, coming through his inadequate language, that Simon momentarily felt a twinge of doubt. Did he believe this? Could it be that it was Connie who had got rid of him, and foisted some kind of death notification on Len? As a super-vicious joke, presumably? He looked at Connie. If she had, then surely there would be some sign on her face of that secret knowledge—some hugging to herself of what she had done all those years ago. But there wasn't. There was nothing in her look but sheer contempt. Len must be acting—acting out grief for a child he had himself got rid of. Got rid of, surely, because he had seen too much.

Suddenly Simon's weakness gave way to a desire to retch. All he wanted to do was get away from this house, these people. His people. Suddenly he wanted to make acknowledgement that his people were those who had made themselves his people, and that these were nothing to him.

'I'll leave you to yourselves,' he said. 'As Teddy said, keeping yourselves to yourselves could be the Simmeter family motto. Perhaps it's that that's really your punishment.'

Half an hour later he had packed his cases, and stuffed things into a couple of carrier bags he had picked up in shops. They represented all of himself that he'd brought to the Simmeters'. As he left the house he heard raised voices from back in the living-room. The recriminations were just starting. The Simmeters had turned in on themselves.

Twenty minutes later he was booking into his old hotel, off New Oxford Street. When he put his head on his pillow, he went straight off into the soundest and most trouble-free sleep he had enjoyed for weeks.

CHAPTER 15

In the week that followed Simon spent all his free hours looking at flats. He was happy and busy; his mind became imperceptibly adjusted to thinking of the future, and occupied itself less with the Simmeters. When he went to bed on Thursday night he was surprised to realize that he had not thought of them once that day. On Friday he got the key for a flat in Swiss Cottage, where he was to remain very happily until 1970, three years after he had married Rosemary.

That weekend he went down to Yeasdon. He had phoned often since he came down from Leeds, but he had never been home. Home had never meshed in his mind with what he had been doing: embedded in his mind was the idea that his investigations held the seed of disloyalty to the Cutheridges. Now he was done with them, and the awkwardness was gone. He had a warm and delighted homecoming, and Dot Cutheridge was over the moon that he looked fit, happy, and well over the miseries of his marriage and separation.

'You look a new man,' she said. 'Practically a teenager again. I bet you've met somebody.'

'Well, there is somebody,' Simon said. 'I don't suppose it will come to anything, so don't start building castles. I'm certainly not going to rush in this time.'

'I didn't notice you rushed in last time,' said Dot, with a countrywoman's tartness. She had never let that incredible gift of a family rob her of common sense in her treatment of Simon.

The only sadness of the visit was the accelerating failure of his father. From being head stockman he had declined after his accident to being a jobber around the estate, and as he had been able to do less and less, his mental agility had gradually left him. Now he spent much of his day in a dream or a doze. Dot and Simon told him things, drew his attention to changes in the garden, or the approach of autumn; he would nod, or venture a comment, but soon he would retreat quite happily into his dream world, which seemed warm with happy reminiscence, leaving mother and son to talk to each other from their positions on either side of him around the open fire.

'You've been looking into this business of who you are, where you came from, haven't you?' said Dot on Saturday night.

'I don't know why we bother to talk,' said Simon, smiling. 'You always know without asking.'

'And you found out?'

'Yes, I found out . . . most things. I found out as much as I need to know.'

'Were they a nice family?'

'No,' said Simon emphatically. 'Not nice at all.'

'I suppose it wasn't likely they would be. Though your mother had looked after you, I'll give her that.'

'Oh, Mother was different. She must have been quite different. But she died . . . '

'Died in the war?'

Simon did not want to distress her needlessly.

'Yes—died about the time I came here. That must have been why I was sent away.'

'Thank God, at any rate, that I didn't steal you from anybody. I've often wondered whether I didn't put difficulties in the way of them finding out who you were. The thought that I might have robbed some poor soul was awful—but not so awful as the thought of giving you back. I always said to myself that if she'd wanted you back she'd have made some effort. I'll offer up a prayer of thanks in Church tomorrow—and a prayer for her, poor soul. Well, Dad—you'll be wanting your supper, won't you?'

Simon went with his mother to the Methodist Church next day. Dot Cutheridge's prayers for the dead natural

mother of Simon were perhaps rather a departure from
orthodox Methodist practice, and Simon too stepped out of
Wesleyan line by telling his mother after the service that he
was going to call on his friend Mick Malone and take him
for a drink before Sunday dinner.

Mick was now married, and Simon was well-known to
the three exuberant, attractive and none-too-clean children
who made his council house a continual happy bedlam.
Mick, predictably, had married a strong-minded girl who
kept him well under control.

'Mind you're back by quarter past one,' she shouted after
them. 'I need you to carve. And bring me a bottle of light
ale.'

They sat outside the Hound and Hare on a bench in the
sun, and began picking up the pieces of their lives since they
had last met. Simon could talk to Mick about the Simmeters
as he could not talk to his mother. But he found that what
Mick was interested in was the process by which he had
found it all out. The emotional resonances meant nothing
to him, but the story had the same sort of appeal to his mind
as tracing the causes of a fault in an engine. Simon thought
his wondering admiration for his cleverness altogether mis-
placed.

'It all goes back to the day when I recognized where I
had lived,' he said. 'I couldn't have done anything if that
hadn't happened. And when I decided to follow it up,
everything led naturally from there. Even then, if I'd had a
name like Smith or Jones I'd never have got anywhere at
all.'

It was only when they were finishing their second pints
and preparing to get off home that Micky asked:

'And what were they like, then, these Simmeters?'

'I was wondering when you were going to ask that.
Horrible.'

'Well, so what? I told you years ago, I don't think it's
important. Any more than it's important that my mum was
a foul-mouthed harridan. All I think about her is: Thank

God I got shot of her, and was brought up here. If she'd had the bringing up of me a bit longer, she'd have made me something else; but luckily she didn't. I don't think there's any part of me that's hers—nor my real dad's, whoever he may be. If I found out my real dad was Winston Churchill it wouldn't make a blind bit of difference to how I thought of myself. I'm me.'

Now Micky's attitude seemed nothing but common sense. Simon had never found anything of himself in the Simmeters.

'I suppose I ought to think of it like mongrel dogs: you never quite know who the father was.'

'It's not only strays like us who're in that position,' said Mick. 'There's plenty of kids in this village who think they know who their dad is, but they couldn't be more mistaken. You can take my word for that, because in one or two cases the real dad is me.'

'Still,' said Simon, 'with mongrel dogs you always know who the mother is. And I'm glad I know who mine was, and what happened to her, however terrible. I'm quite happy to think that I came out of Len's past like the figure of Revenge. I hope the bastard is writhing at the thought that I might have changed my mind and gone along to the police.'

And when Simon, walking home, had given Mick a brief account of Len, Connie, Teddy and their mother, that was virtually the last of the Simmeters in his life for quite a while. That night he went back to London, to a new flat, a new kind of life. Of course he told Rosemary, when he had dated her a few more times. It was a memorable day, but mostly because later that same evening they slept together for the first time. By then the story of his origins had lost much of its importance for Simon, and Rosie docketed it in her mind as a piece of information about her husband-to-be, but something much lower in her scale of values than what he told her about the Cutheridges, whom he not long afterwards took her to meet. It was many years later, and then almost by accident, that the Simmeters came into Simon's life again.

CHAPTER 16

In May of 1979 Simon Cutheridge took his three children on a motoring tour around Sussex. He took Friday off from the Zoo, where he was now one of the two or three most senior members of the scientific staff. He had promised the children a trip of some kind while their mother was away, and the free Friday made it a leisurely long weekend. Rosemary was now an actress—not exactly a famous one, but the sort of face that, seen on the box, makes people ask: 'Where have I seen her before? What else has she been in?' There had been some rocky and dispiriting years after drama school, but work was now, as she put it, regularly irregular: there were never too many months in a row when she was out of a solid job. And if the worst came to the worst there were television commercials for dog foods or bedtime drinks.

Rosemary's work at the moment was filming a second series of a BBC sit. com. that she had first appeared in three years earlier. Having run the gamut of black boy married to white girl, white boy married to black girl, older man married to younger woman, older woman married to younger man, boy batching in a flat of girls, girl batching in a flat of boys—having run, in fact, through all the drearily predictable ideas that ever were thrown up in script conferences, the BBC had caught its breath and looked through its records to see which of them could possibly justify a second series. Luckily one of the ones they came up with was Rosemary's. This was a sit. com. about a newly divorced couple still living in the same street. Rosemary played the wacky friend of the family who lived in the house in between. Unluckily the series was set—for no apparent reason, except that the writers seemed to believe that a mere mention of

the name would produce a laugh—in Stoke-on-Trent. It
was filmed in the BBC Midlands Studio. Rosemary had to
be away for three solid blocks of three weeks at a time.

'It's crumby, but it's bread, and it keeps my face before
the great British public,' she said philosophically, as she
went through the script of the first episode, trying to sharpen
up her wacky wisecracks.

So that May Simon took his children through the Downs
and villages of Sussex. The car was in a state of continual
song, laughter and uproar. Mrs Thatcher had just become
Prime Minister, and his second child, Emily—the apple of
his eye, and the one who most strikingly took after their
mother—was making a speciality of imitating her. 'Where
there was strife, let there be concord,' she would intone,
in high, breathy tones of manifest insincerity. It was a
performance that Simon thought by no means bad for a
ten-year-old.

It was Saturday afternoon, a blowy, exhilarating day, and
Martin, the youngest, was navigating because he said it was
the boy's job to. For once this was not disputed, since
nobody else wanted to do it, but Martin made his job more
difficult by continually reading the maps the wrong way up.
Luckily none of them had any clear idea of where they
wanted to go.

'We go where the fancy takes us,' said Simon.

'We go where Martin's lousy map-reading lands us up,'
said Angela, the eldest. 'What's the signpost say?'

'It must be Lytton Magna,' said Martin.

'Well, it isn't: it's Cattermole,' said Emily.

Simon swerved to the left, and took the road to
Cattermole.

'What did you do that for, Daddy? I don't think I like
the name Cattermole. Is there anything special there?'

'I've heard of it somewhere,' said Simon. 'What does it
say in the AA Book, Martin?'

After much hedging and muttering Martin found the
entry and read out: 'A village of no special charm or charac-

ter. Pop. 1,700.'

'Those are the best kind of villages,' said Emily wisely.
They're not all spoilt and touristy.'

'What's wrong with being touristy?' demanded Martin.
We're tourists. And at least you get good ice-cream in
touristy places. Why should we go to a village of no special
charm or character?'

'To see if we can spot the charm or character the man
who wrote that missed,' said Simon.

As it turned out the children were easily placated, once
they'd parked the car and found a sweets and ice-cream
shop that satisfied even Martin's exacting requirements.
Before they'd been in Cattermole long they became preoccupied with some business or game of their own, and Simon
was free to stroll on ahead of them, trying to remember the
scraps of detail about Cattermole that he had learnt so long
ago.

Blenheim Avenue—that was it. The number he could not
for the life of him remember. But when he found Blenheim
Avenue, most of it had been rebuilt in matchstick-Georgian
style by a firm of wholesale home-packagers who had made
shoddy whole tracts of Southern England. The house that
his mother had come to, prospecting for a refuge for him
from the bombs, was no more.

Simon walked curiously through the village. Of course it
aroused in him no memories—how could it? He certainly
hadn't been with his mother when she wrote, because she
had sent him her love. But it was curious to think that—but
for the exceptional and unlucky violence of Len that May
night—it was here that he might have spent his early years,
rather than Yeasdon. Cattermole had a dry, elderly, unin-
spiring whiff to it: it reminded him of a candle that has never
burnt well, and shows signs of shortly going out. Simon, not
for the first time, felt he had been lucky. In every way
Yeasdon had been preferable to this.

The church was a little apart from the centre of the village.
It was a standard, solid, Perpendicular construction, which

the AA Book would doubtless also say had no particular
character or charm. Simon turned aside from the road and
wandered into the churchyard.

'What are you going in there for?' demanded Emily.

'If you want to get to know a place, you have to look at
the churchyard,' pontificated Simon.

'How? Why? What do we look for?'

Simon was a bit nonplussed.

'You look at the gravestones,' he said.

Luckily the children returned to their game, and let him
wander and browse. The dutiful wives and mothers, the
dearly beloved husbands, the sons and daughters of the
above, passed across his vision—many of them of exemplary
piety, some long-suffering in illness, others steadfast in faith.
'All the little lies of village life,' said Simon to himself. Surely
gravestones held the highest proportion of written untruth,
outside of the popular press.

'Looking for someone special?' said an old voice behind
him. Simon jumped and looked round, surprised out of a
dream. It was a gnarled, ill-shaven face, with sharp, bright
eyes, and wearing labourer's clothes—the trousers tied
round the cracked boots with string.

'David Simmeter,' said Simon.

'Over there,' said the old man, pointing. 'Down by
the east wall. Through there, see. A bit to your left. I
know them all, I do. Further left. There he is. That's
him.'

Like a somnambulist Simon had walked on. Past more
dearly beloved husbands, spinsters of exemplary piety, sons
and daughters who had died in childhood. And then he
stood, shivering in the blustery wind, down by the east
wall—the voice of the old man, and the voices of his laughing
children, coming to him across the churchyard. And he
knelt down in front of a squat, square tombstone, with
incrustations of moss at its foot, dry bits of twig and leaf
clinging to it from last autumn. And on the stone he
read:

IN LOVING MEMORY
OF
DAVID SIMMETER (1938-1941)
CHERISHED SON OF
LEONARD AND MARY SIMMETER
KILLED IN AN AIR RAID ON THIS PARISH, JUNE 1941.
TAKEN EARLY.

Simon stood in the wind, looking on and on at this witness to his own early death.

'Little boy a relative of yours?'

The old man had come over, and stood looking curiously at him from a few feet away, with an air of respectfully wondering whether there might be anything in it for him.

'I—yes. Yes, I think so. Do you remember him?'

'Not him. Not the little lad. But I remember the burial. Naturally I do, because I dug the grave. Didn't go to the war, on account of my chest.' The old man wheezed, as if to give evidence, but he chuckled proudly. 'Hasn't stopped me living to seventy-five, though, has it? 'Course, nowadays I only tidy up the place a bit. Arthritic—terrible place for arthritis is Cattermole. But I dug all the graves, nigh on, from 'forty to 'sixty-nine. I'm the man to come to if you've a fancy to find out about graves!'

'So you dug this one?'

'Like I said. This was one of my first. I remember because we didn't have so many air raid deaths here in Cattermole. We were that bit off the routes them Narzi bombers took. But that time we were for it. That time we had the three.'

'Three?'

'There was the elderly couple as were looking after him. Over there, they are. All killed by the same bomb. He'd only been there a couple of months, the little kid. And by all accounts he was a nice, well-spoken lad—not like some. Dirty, foul-mouthed little ruffians we had down here, and some of the mothers were no better. The Templetons were going around saying they'd been very lucky. And then they all gets blown to smithereens. Makes you think, don't it?'

'Do you remember the funeral?'

'Oh aye. They were all the same day. The Templetons had children and grandchildren, and they were there for the funeral, or some of them were. But for the little boy there was just the father. *He* nearly wasn't there either, because he'd recently moved house, and they had difficulty contacting him.'

'You remember him, do you?'

'I do that. Because he were in such a taking on. Thin, nervy type—not the sort you'd take to. Twitching and shaking he were, right through the service. And when we started heaving the earth in, he burst out into such a cry—sobbing and shaking he were. But there—they said the gent had lost his wife, similar, only a few weeks before, so it's not surprising he took on. I always remember that funeral, because it was one of my first, and because we didn't have many air raid victims in Cattermole, like I said. And then the father being so shook up, like he was close to a breakdown. Did you say you were a relative?'

'*Daddy*!' came imperative voices from over by the church. 'What are you doing? Come *on*. There's nothing here.'

'Yes,' said Simon. 'I am some sort of relative.'

He fumbled in his pocket, and could find only a five-pound note. He handed it to the old man, and turned away, bewildered.

'Well, that's very generous, sir. Very kind indeed. I'll see the grave is kept clean and tidy . . . '

Simon walked back to his children in a dream. He called them together and began shepherding them towards the car.

'What's the *matter*, Daddy? Why do you look so white and funny? Are you ill?'

'I don't think so, darling. Perhaps it was the pub lunch I ate.'

'Pub lunches can be *very* strange and awful,' said Emily authoritatively.

'Did you discover the life of the village from the gravestones?' demanded Martin.

'Something like that,' said Simon.

'That seems funny,' said Martin. 'Since they're dead.'

'All the dead were once alive,' said Simon solemnly.

'Except stillborn children,' said Angela.

'Which was the one you were looking at for ages?' asked Emily.

'A little boy I once knew,' said her father, starting the car. 'He is dead, and once had been alive.'

When Simon and the children got back on Sunday evening to the house in Highgate where they now lived, it was a long time before he could get the children to bed. First there were the pets to be collected from the neighbours. Then they demanded to ring their mother in Birmingham. All the children had to talk to her about their jaunt, and it was a long time before Simon could get a word in. Rosemary was feeling jaundiced.

'The series will be appalling,' she announced. 'The mixture as before, with water, and yet more water. Last time they had three good jokes per episode, plus a lot of dialogue you were supposed to say as though it was funny. This time it's two good or not-so-good jokes, plus acres of padding. The two principals are just going through the motions, and so, frankly, am I . . . '

Cheering Rosemary up took some time, and then he had to make Ovaltine for the children; they all insisted on taking their pets to bed, because they said they were moping. Finally he let them, turned off their lights, heard their last calls to each other and their laughter, and went downstairs and poured himself a whisky.

When he had sat thinking in a chair for some minutes, he got up and went into his study. The notebooks he had kept in 1964 were at the bottom of a desk drawer—underneath a sheaf of Zoo committee minutes, administrative memos, financial statements. He had not looked inside the notebooks since the family had moved house in 1970. Then, he remembered, he had flicked through them, shaken his head at his intense absorption of six years before, and then gone on with the task of getting the house in order. Could he not treat them in the same off-hand manner now? But the exercise books looked up at him—browning, faded, musty: a laborious record of a maladroit exercise in detection.

One thing had become incontrovertible, he thought, since his visit to the churchyard. If David Simméter had been born in 1938, then he could not be that David Simmeter. Nobody had been very sure of his age that day when he arrived on the platform at Yeasdon Station, but he most certainly had been more than three. Between five and six, Dot had thought, and Dot knew about these things. He felt himself, when he thought back to that memory of arriving, to be more than three; he *knew* himself to have been older than three. And as he leafed his way through the notebooks he began to remark on things he should have picked up at the time.

'Everyone's talking about someone younger than I would have been,' he said to himself.

The man who had known Len in the 'thirties, the fellow Fascist, had talked about a meeting Len addressed just before the war: he had said that Len had made his mother—David Simmeter's mother—hold him up before the crowd. And he'd been 'hardly more than a babby', the man had said. But he, Simon, would have been decidedly more than a baby. He noted that Len had said the picture of mother and son that adorned their living-room was taken after the war began. But the little boy clinging to his mother's skirts was too young to be him, Simon, if it was taken in, say, May 1940. Of course David Simmeter must have been born in 1938. 'Worrying times to bring a new soul into the world,' his mother had said when she was pregnant. She would hardly have said that so feelingly back in 1935 or 6. In fact, thinking back on it, the tone of everyone's remarks about Davey Simmeter was the tone of someone discussing a little boy, not the serious five-year-old Simon himself had been when he arrived in Yeasdon.

Simon remembered the anguish in Len's voice when he had talked about his little son, killed when he was little more than three; he remembered the wail as he said, 'Talk about punishment!' The anguish, the wail, had been genuine.

'I suppose Fascists have feelings,' said Simon.

He went and poured himself another drink, and put Mahler's Fourth on the gramophone. Walking round the room, as the music yearned around him, he said to himself: 'I must get rid of preconceptions. I must wipe the slate clean. I must think things through from the beginning.'

Then he sat down and went back to his notebooks. He went through them once more, word by word, from the beginning. He read his account of what he had learned from the old man in the Paddington pub. 'He'd come out after watching *Coronation Street,*' Simon remembered. 'I expect he still does.' He read over his account of his talks with Connie and Teddy, the long chat over coffee in Paddington with the Mosley admirer from way back, then his much scrappier account of that last dismal party with all the Simmeters together. 'I was losing interest then,' said Simon to himself.

The notebooks were nearing an end when he came to Mary Simmeter's letter from Cattermole. I tried hard with that, Simon remembered. It had been in his old hotel near New Oxford Street; he'd checked in there after banging out of the house in Miswell Terrace. He had sat next morning over his notebooks, trying to set down the letter as nearly verbatim as he could manage. His memory had been well-trained by then: it had honed itself to highlight every detail that he heard or saw that might be of relevance to the questions of Mary and David Simmeter. He thought he had got down that letter very nearly as Mary Simmeter had written it.

And as he sat there in his chair, with an ethereal soprano voice singing of the paradisal delights of childhood filling the room, he had the glimmering of an idea. He thought he saw. At last he thought he understood.

CHAPTER 17

Islington had changed beyond recognition. Stone by stone it might not be very different, but in all the inessentials it had undergone the sort of face-lift that restores an uncertain glamour to elderly Americans. As with the face-lift, the effect was oddly nonplussing (for what does one say, after all, to a woman who has renovated her face since one last saw her?) Everything was familiar yet unfamiliar. Simon had been back for the opera once or twice, but since the company had moved from Sadler's Wells to the dreary and unwelcoming vastness of the Coliseum he had not been there at all. Islington had bloomed. Doors and window-frames were flaunting bright colours, window-boxes and tubs of flowers abounded, bright floral curtains and bold Scandinavian ones graced the windows, and sharp dressers walked confidently up to their front doors, to be greeted by precocious children in neo-Victorian outfits. Grafted on to the native Islington stock, it seemed, was a new shoot of media people, of intellectuals, and fringe upper-classes. One would not be surprised to come upon Margaret Drabble whitening a front doorstep.

Next door to 25 Miswell Terrace—Simon hugely enjoyed the development—lived a West Indian family. The incredibly smart lady who came out of the front door of No. 23 just as he was ringing the bell of 25 had a face he vaguely remembered: did she front a programme for immigrants on Channel 2? She had the sort of confidence (Simon knew it from Rosemary) that comes from possessing a face that people feel they know.

'She'll be down the Colonel Monk,' the woman said. 'Always is in the early evening.'

Did people talk to their neighbours now?

Simon said experimentally: 'Connie?'

'That's right,' said the woman over her shoulder. 'Likes her three gin and t's in the evening. Buy her one of them and you're a friend for life.'

She marched off towards the tube, all brown leather and shiny brown skin. Simon looked at his watch. He had got about two and a half hours. A neighbour was taking his and her own children to a rerun of *The Railway Children*, and though it was the sixth time of seeing in the case of his own brood, he could rely on their enjoying an hour's discussion of the finer points afterwards before they would want to get back into their own home. He set off in the direction of the Colonel Monk.

Change in the Colonel Monk could only be for the better. Simon looked without disapproval at the green imitation leather, the bogus brass, the prints of Restoration London, the photocopied broadsheets and Wanted notices. Anything that chased away the dimness that was there before had to be an improvement, and the buxom Australian girls behind the bar were un-Restoration but much to be preferred to the surly Mine Host he had known. Less of an improvement were the clientele. Glossy smartness was the norm, and voices were sharpened to command attention. 'As I said to the D.-G.' floated through the smoke and fumes, and, 'Margaret's made a good start, but Willie thinks she needs to be kept on a tight rein.' Above the clinking of glasses could be heard the clinking of dropped names—the counterfeit coinage of asserted self-importance, the banners flourished against the ignominy of knowing, and therefore being, nobody.

In such company it was not difficult to pick out Connie Simmeter. Even her age marked her off, for the Colonel Monk was no longer territory for old people. Her size did too, for the pub was full of pencil-slim people who converted food and drink into instant energy for self-advancement. Connie Simmeter, on the other hand, had followed the example of her mother and grown mountainous with age. She would have looked fat anywhere, but here she looked like a sack of potatoes in a field of corn. The sort of synthetic-fabric smartness she had once affected was impossible for her now: the hoops and bulges of her fleshiness could no longer be constricted into order and form. They simply had to be covered, and Connie seemed no longer to take any interest in the covering. She sat over her gin and tonic, but if Simon's first thoughts were of her mother, he realized quickly that there was a difference: Connie seemed to gaze out on the world with complacency, even with amiability. 'I am mingling with Names,' her demeanour seemed to proclaim, 'or at any rate observing them from the sidelines.' From behind pudgy cheeks the eyes darted about, but they passed over Simon with no sign of interest or recognition. He paid for his glass of wine to the girl with the Broken Hill accent, and made in the direction of her table.

'It's Miss Simmeter, isn't it? Connie?'

She was sitting at a little table on her own, her bulk spread over the cushions of a window seat. She looked up expectantly, as if prepared to welcome any diversion, forgive any intrusion.

'I don't think I—wait a minute. Goodness me—I *do* remember you. Give me a moment . . . You weren't one of the young men at Peter Jones's, were you? No—they'd have called me Constance. Wait. It's coming back to me. You were one of the lodgers. Of course! Mr Cutheridge! To think of me forgetting. I mentioned your name so often after you left. I suppose you can guess why. To turn the screws on Len, of course! What laughs I had about that! Fancy you catching up with Len after all those years . . . But there, I called you Mr Cutheridge, but I suppose Cutheridge isn't your real name, is it?'

"Your glass is empty,' said Simon, side-stepping, and conscious of the neighbour's injunction. 'Won't you let me get you another? It's gin and tonic, isn't it?'

'How kind. Very gentlemanly. But you always were. Not many gentlemen around these days. Yes, gin and t, please. Catches up with all of us in the end, doesn't it?'

Unsure what this last remark meant, but suspecting it was the gin and tonic that did the catching, Simon fetched her another. He sat down companionably opposite her, and watched her put the tonic in, which she did with a careful hand.

'Mustn't drown it,' she said, leaning back contentedly. 'In the neighbourhood, are you? Visiting? Where do you live now? Highgate! Oh—a very nice address. I had a gentleman friend in Highgate once. I'd like to move myself, but you can't get up the energy when you're my age. Still, I must say the neighbourhood is looking up. I expect you've noticed. Some of the people who come here are *very highly placed*. And I've got everything as I like it now in Miswell Terrace.'

'You're on your own there now, are you?'

'Oh yes, long since. Apart from the lodgers, of course. Very useful the money is, now that we can charge an economic rent. The old age p. wouldn't keep me in the style I expect, I can tell you.'

'So the rest of the family died, did they?'

'Except Teddy. Mother went not long after that night you were there, the night she fell. Something internal—I forget the details. She lasted a few months, in and out of hospital, but she was a complete invalid. Her time was up, even she knew that. Well into extra time, if you ask me, but then Ma and I never did hit it off. Then there was Len. It must have been—let me see—about '69 or '70 when Len went. Well, not so much went as was pushed, in my opinion.'

'Pushed?'

'Officially it was an accident.' Connie edged her bosom confidentially forward over the table, looking immensely knowing. 'Fell in front of a Tube train. The coroner didn't seem to have any doubts, so who was I to raise a stink? I got the money from Ma and the house from Len, so I was laughing. But I ask you: Len had worked in the Underground most of his life. He wasn't going to fall accidentally in front of a train. Of course, there was the possibility of suicide: Len hadn't been happy those last years of his life.'

'No?'

Connie giggled.

'You can guess the reason, because it was thanks to you, mostly. But still, I *knew* it couldn't be suicide, because I knew Len. He'd never have had the nerve. They say bullies are always cowards. I have my doubts, because in her prime Ma was one without being the other. But Len, now: he was both. Thank God. Because he'd have been the world's nastiest bully if it hadn't been that he was yellow to the core. Len would never have been brave enough to chuck himself in front of a train.'

'But who on earth would push him?'

'Think! You knew all about him, didn't you? He wasn't liked at work, you know, and that's putting it mildly.' She leaned forward again, putting forward her theory with a relish that amounted to gloating. 'It's my belief one of the blackies working on the Underground pushed him. God bless him! Though it could equally be one of the whites. There were plenty of those that hated him for his politics. And Len was just naturally unlikeable, let's face it.'

'You don't seem to dislike the idea.'

Connie wobbled back in her seat and smiled a smile of immense complacency.

'Why should I? I'm afraid I'm not a hypocrite. I say what I think. I'd nothing to be grateful to Len for. It was the same with him as with Mother: there wasn't a soul to mourn them. And of course I got the house!'

'That was lucky,' said Simon. He did not bother with genteel circumlocutions, since Connie so obviously rejected them.

'Yes, wasn't it? He left no will, and Teddy said he didn't want any Simmeter property. He's retired now, by the way, and living very comfortably in Southsea. He's got a wife, you see, and one of the kids is still with them, so Teddy's lucky. Deserves it, though. He comes to see me every time he comes to London.'

'So everything has worked out nicely for you. I'm glad.'

'Not at all bad. Not that I've *enough* money, mind, but I didn't squander what I got from Ma, and then with the income from the lodgers, I can get most of the things I want.' She gave Simon a roguish wink. 'In the material line, anyway! If I go careful the money will see me out. Thanks, I will have another, since you're so kind.'

When Simon returned with the means to retank her, he said:

'So Len's last years weren't happy, then?'

'No. And why should they be? I never moved out—kept meaning to, but never summoned up the energy. So we were both living together. He'd have liked to have me slaving away for him in the house, like Mary used to, but I could always scare the living daylights out of him just by mentioning your name. After all those years, when he thought the whole business was buried deeper than Australia, to have you pop up and point the finger! Marvellous!' She chuckled appreciatively. 'I do think you were clever to find it all out!'

'Oh, I don't know about that,' said Simon, sitting back easily in his chair, and watching her. 'I certainly wouldn't say I'd got to the bottom of the business then.'

'I thought you did pretty well!' The chuckle changed to a vengeful laugh. 'And Len thought you did a pretty thorough job too!'

'But really there were big gaps in what I knew,' said Simon easily, hoping that to tease her out would be more effective than accusing her. 'For example, I knew nothing about Ted.'

Connie looked up at him sharply, but on consideration she relaxed over her gin, scarcely less pleased with herself than before.

'I don't see there was any need for you to know anything about Ted.'

'He was in the house, all the period we were discussing. I think it's funny nobody ever mentioned him.'

'He *wasn't* mentioned much—even while he was there.
After he'd gone we hardly mentioned him at all. Naturally,
I'd have thought. Anyway, you Spurlings knew all about
him.'

'I didn't. I should have realized when I read that letter
of Mary's, where she sent her love to Ted. Not Teddy.
Nobody ever seems to have called your brother Ted. And
by 1941 he wouldn't have been at home—especially spring
'41. He'd have been up in the air, flying planes.'

'That's right. He was. Things might have been better if
he had been at home. You're right—we did call the boy
Ted, to make the difference. I *am* surprised you didn't know
about him. After all the fuss you Spurlings made when he
was on the way!'

Simon chanced his arm.

'Because he was illegitimate?'

'Of course.' Her eyes clouded over, and a bitter expression
took possession of her normally good-humoured face. 'You
young people: you've no idea what it was like then! The
shame we were supposed to feel ... And the Spurlings
being chapel people as well—that made it a real scandal,
something only talked about at home, under their breaths.
Teddy told me that as soon as they got whisper they were
round at Farrow Street, demanding that I keep away from
the district, and that I call myself Mrs. You'd have thought
one or the other would have done, wouldn't you?'

'They were worse than your own family?'

'Oh, Ma and Len were bad enough. The fuss! They
offered me a weekly pittance to stay away, and when I said
I'd come round to discuss it, Ma said, "Then you come
after dark!" It was a real laugh, that meeting. I remember
when they put it to me that I should take a married
name—I'd been going to, anyway—I said: "All right. I'll
take a married name. I'll take the name of the father. I'll
call myself Mrs Mandel." Len blew his top! I really got a
kick out of that. I felt I'd held my own.'

A firework rose and bloomed into showers of sparkles in

Simon's brain. Ted Mandel. Edward Mandel. I know it. I remember it. It says something to me, as David Simmeter never did. I was Edward Mandel . . . I *am* not Edward Mandel, but I *was* him.

Connie had not noticed his reaction. She had interrupted her reminiscences to attend to her drink, with an old person's eagerness for the comforts of the present.

'But why,' Simon asked, curious, 'should Len blow his top?'

'The name: Mandel. I remember he shouted: "But that's a Jewish name!" And I said: "Not so bloody surprising, since he's a Jewish boy." All hell broke loose. Len kept wailing: "You're having a Jewish baby!" and I'd say: "Technically speaking, I'd say I have half shares in him." Whenever Len or Ma said the word "Jewish", they hissed it—in case the neighbours heard.'

'Who was he, the father?'

'He was the son of the family I worked for. Nice enough boy—a year younger than me. I left home, you see, round about 1932. Went to work in a shop first, and had a room nearby. I got in with this young left-wing crowd—very idealistic, you know. I suppose you'd call it a reaction against Len and Ma. Well, I always wanted to better myself—would have done, too, if the brat hadn't come along— and one of this crowd got me this job doing secretarial work, which was a step up, though not much of one. It was an organization to aid refugees from Nazi Germany. Really it was rich Jews here helping to get Jews out of Germany, but they tried to make it more general, played down that side of it, because there were plenty of people in the Conservative Party at the time who were pretty much of Len's way of thinking. So it suited them to employ a non-Jew. They were good people on the whole, but nobody's fools.'

'I begin to understand,' said Simon. 'I think I get it.'

'So I was working at the Mandels' all day. They ran a chain of jewellers', but the committee I worked for operated

from their home. The parents were mostly out during the
day, and the boy—Isaiah was his name, would you believe
it?—had just finished with school. He was eighteen or so. I
suppose you could say that what happened was pretty much
inevitable.'

'And I imagine his family was less than pleased.'

'You're not wrong!' Connie's mouth twisted with contempt. 'See them letting their bright boy marry out of the
faith! They packed him off to Edinburgh University—
further away than Oxford.' Her face relaxed once more into
its usual flaccid contentment. 'Though if the truth were
known, there was never much of what you'd call love between us. He was too fly to be easily caught, parents or no
parents. Anyway, I was paid off. And I made them pay,
and pay well! Otherwise I'd never have had the brat, or I'd
have had it adopted. I thought it was my passport to the
good life. Mind you, if I'd *known* the trouble a kid causes!
. . . I was too green, that was my trouble.'

'But you had two supplies of money coming in, though.'

'That's right. I never told Len and Ma about the money
I was getting from the Mandels, or they'd have cut off their
subsidy. Tainted lucre! I had a little flat in Peckham, had
the baby (January 28th, 1936, the day the old King was
buried), and all in all I wasn't too badly off. If it hadn't
been for the baby I'd have been fine.'

'You didn't care for him?'

'I *cared* for him, in one sense; there was no one else to. I
didn't *like* him. I can't imagine why women want babies.
They ruin your life. I know Ted ruined mine.'

'Why did you decide to go back to your family?'

'I was afraid. It was as simple as that. It was early in the
summer of '39. Everyone was talking about the coming war.
I used to see Teddy once a week, when he brought the
money from the family. He was a brick, Teddy was—that's
why I named the boy after him. Well, with all this talk I
got scared to death—invasion, air raids, occupation, that
was all anyone thought about. And me alone in a tiny flat,

with a kid to look after, and not a friend in the world. I put out feelers through Teddy, and got back the gracious message from Ma that it would be all right to move back if I called myself *Mrs* Mandel, and wore a wedding-ring. We'd all say my husband died. And that's what we did. At least there was somebody *there*, near me. I wasn't alone.'

'I'd have thought it must have been a pretty unpleasant atmosphere to go back to.'

Connie shrugged, and smiled her complacent smile.

'Water off a duck's back. I can ignore that sort of thing. I never liked fending for myself, you know. Slaving away to get meals, keep the little bugger clean and tidy—that wasn't my line at all. And at home was Mary, just waiting to be the substitute mother. That suited me down to the ground. And I don't mind telling you there was another reason: I thought that if Jerry *did* come over, it might be useful being Len's sister. I make no bones about thinking of my own skin first.'

'But it didn't work out very well, I take it.'

'Oh, not at all bad. From my point of view. It took most of the load off my shoulders. There was just the problem of Ted.'

'I suppose,' said Simon, cautiously exploring an area of half-memory, 'that it was mostly about Ted that Mary and Len argued—fought—in those years. You kept that from me before.'

Connie chuckled in rich and careless reminiscence.

'Was it ever! From the beginning Len could hardly bear the sight of him. A Jewish boy in his house! Playing with his David! He tried to banish him from *his* part of the house, but it didn't work out. *I* wasn't interested in him; *I* wasn't going to have him clinging to my skirts all day. I'd moved back to see an end to that. So of course Mary had to look after him: she wasn't one to see a child moping and neglected and do nothing about it. So back Ted would be in Len's part of the house, as he called it. The looks he gave! If looks could kill! . . . '

'He didn't actually mistreat him?'

'He would have. He would have liked to. But Mary always stood in the way.'

'Physically?'

'Eventually that. First she said she'd go to the police if there was any brutality. Then she threatened to take Davey and go and live with her family. Her dad was dead—stiff-necked old bugger—but she had a whole host of brothers and sisters, as you know. That got through to Len, because of course Mary would have got custody of the child if there'd been any sort of separation. Gradually, though, he realized that Mary would never leave Ted in the same house as him. Funny woman . . . I never understood her . . . What was Ted to her? But she washed and cleaned for him, darned his clothes, till he was as well-turned-out as her David. I suppose some women just love kids. But it doesn't seem natural.'

'And when he couldn't take it out on . . . on Ted, he started taking it out on Mary?'

'That's it. Typical Len. First the odd cuff around the head, then real blows. Always about Ted. "The Yid bastard", as Len used to call him. Sometimes it happened when he was there. Once or twice I caught him at night, listening on the stairs. The expression on that child's face! Well, I'm not sentimental, but it got through to me, I can tell you. He had nightmares about it. I know that because he slept in the next room to mine. Screamed out, moaned. I always let him have them out . . . They say it's better.'

A picture was forming: tiny sparks of memory were igniting, and illuminating dark corners of Simon's mind. The boy on the stairs, listening to the thumps and cries of fighting adults. The boy in bed, having his nightmare out, waking up drenched not in urine but in sweat. The boy in the hostile house, keeping out of sight of most of the members of it, with one badgered, beaten protector. The picture was forming slowly in his mind, as on an old, worn-out television set. But the lazy, scattered picture was helping him to understand that later picture: the little boy arriving at Yeasdon Station, determined to find a new family, new protectors.

'What about that night?' he asked. 'The night of Mary's death.'

Connie pursed up her mouth, as if at a distasteful memory.

'Oh—that night. We told you about that. But it wasn't just that night—it was all the nights leading up to it. Weeks. Months.' She passed her hand across her forehead, and in remembering that time she displayed for the only time in Simon's acquaintance with her some crack in the carapace of confidence that enveloped her. She was remembering fear, blank terror. 'Raids, raids, raid. Sirens, trips to the shelter, to the Underground. People huddling on the stairs, the platforms, along the corridors. Explosions . . . fires. Every time you came out, you looked to see what was gone. It was like hell on earth, and it went on and on . . . ' Slowly her complacency returned. 'I think it was a miracle I kept my head that night, I really do.'

'Len, I suppose, lost his?'

'Well and truly. He'd been cracking up for weeks. If they were coming, why didn't they come? If Britain was going to be bombed into surrender, why didn't we surrender? One of his best friends in the British Union had just been interned. Would he be next? In April he sent little David to Sussex. That was the beginning of the end between him and Mary. Now Ma was his only ally in the house, and she wasn't exactly a comforting body. Then that night he seemed to go over the top.'

'What was it about?'

'Funny thing is, I can't remember. We'd been in the shelter, I remember that, and had come out after the all-clear, about half past ten. We saw that houses in the area had been bombed. Mary put Ted to bed, and came down again, and then it all blew up. She'd lost the battle over David, because she half thought Len was right, that he ought to be in the country. Now she gave whatever strength she had to defend Ted. To tell you the truth, I think it was about nothing. That's often the way, isn't it? It was something like Len using Ted's ration card to buy extra sweets for Ma—some fiddling thing like that. Ma always liked her sweet things, and never got enough of them during the war. But however it started, it developed into a real slanging match—Len going on about Yids, Mary about greed and heartlessness. Davey not being there gave Mary courage, I think: he was out of the battle. I do remember her telling Ma to her face she was greedy, and that took nerve, I can tell you. She was quite able to defend herself, of course, but Len charged in, all synthetic outrage at the insult to his mother, and soon there were blows as usual . . . Then suddenly Mary was on the floor.'

'Dead?'

'Yes. We didn't find out for a few minutes. I remember saying: "You ought to be ashamed. Go and make her a cup of tea, Ma." But when Ma had put the kettle on, she still hadn't stirred. Len was looking at her, hopping from one foot to the other, his red, bleary little eyes all wide with fear. Then we found she was dead, and Ma decided what we had to do.'

'I might have guessed she'd arranged it all.'

'Oh yes—trust Ma. *She* wouldn't lose her head in a crisis, not Ma. First she went and found this bombed house that the ARP and fire people hadn't got to yet. Then she and I and Len took Mary there—' Connie shivered, and drew a large old woollen cardigan round her shoulders—'carrying her between us, like she was wounded, or drunk, through those pitch-dark streets. We just left her there, in the sitting-room, with the other dead. We told the police later that she'd been worried about some friends she'd made, who'd only recently moved there, and had gone to see them just before the raid. It was really quite convincing, thanks mostly to Ma. It was only much later, when I found out who they were, that I thought the Jews really did have a habit of catching up with Len. Anyway, all the time we were carrying her there, her arms around our shoulders, like she was walking with difficulty, all the way there I was thinking and thinking . . . And as I say, I'm proud I didn't lose my head.'

'Thinking? What do you mean? What about?'

'Ted, of course.' Connie smiled at Simon, a secret little smile, almost conspiratorial. We're both men and women of the world, it seemed to say. 'Doesn't do any harm to tell now, it being so long ago. I was thinking of me being lumbered with Ted again, now Mary was gone. Just when I was thinking of doing some light war work, getting out a bit more. I did that later, you know: worked near an American air base in Norfolk. Had some times, I can tell you! And here was Mary dying on me, leaving me lumbered with the kid again . . . So I was thinking. And what I did was quite clever. Really very cunning, though I say it myself.'

'What did you do?'

She edged forward the whole heavy top of her body across the table, and there suffused her face a slow smile of the most complete and cloudless self-approbation.

'As soon as we got back to Farrow Street, I said to Len: "You do realize, don't you, that Ted was sitting at the top of the stairs. He must have heard everything." '

'Had he been?'

'Not that I know of. That was the beauty of it! The cunning! Though of course he *had* heard them often enough, and Len knew it. He went wild, practically off his head. "He'll have to be got rid of," he kept saying. Just like one of those old melodramas. I wanted to laugh. "You're not planning on killing two people in one night, are you, Len?" I said. But he was quite mad—hissing it out, in case the neighbours were still up. Children were all the same, he said. If the police really leaned on them, they couldn't keep things quiet. Ted had it in for him, Len said. "Did you think he ought to have a special place in his heart for you?" I asked. Len got wilder and wilder, just like I intended. Ted would blab what he knew just to spite him, Len said. Ma was getting pretty worried too—I liked that: Ma, the human whalebone, almost getting jittery! And when they were both in a proper old tizz-wozz, up I came with the solution: "We can get rid of him without killing him," I said.'

'How would you do that, then?' asked Simon ingenuously.

'Easy! I said to Len: "Look, there's parties of evacuee kids going off to the country every day from Paddington. If we get at him tomorrow morning, put the fear of the devil into him, tell him he's to tell no one who he is, or where he comes from, then we can attach him to one of those groups going off tomorrow, and we'll have seen the last of him. Suits you, and it certainly suits me!'

'How clever,' said Simon, admiringly. 'That was really smart.' That was obviously Connie's opinion too. She smiled at him triumphantly. 'And is that what you did?'

'That's exactly what we did. It *was* a bit wicked, thinking back on it, but wasn't it ingenious? Next morning we got him up early. Ma was cleaning up all traces of the fight. I let Len do most of the initial stuff, so if it all came out I could say I only went along with it to shield Len. That way I was covered. Len told him he was to go away. Something terrible had happened. He was to keep who he was an absolute secret, with some pretty graphic threats as to what would happen if he didn't. He was not to tell anybody anything about himself. He was to lie, make up whatever he fancied, but if he told them who he was—well, you know the sort of thing you terrify kids with.'

'But it was a hell of a risk, wasn't it?'

'But Len thought he would be *more* of a risk if he stayed. And I had a line of retreat open. It all came together so beautifully. I remember later on, sitting in his little room, and he and I were bundling some of his things—God knows what, I hardly knew what was going on—into a little case and a satchel. And he said: "What is it that's happened? Is it Auntie Mary?" And I said: "No, she's just gone away to visit Davey. It was to do with the war." That seemed to satisfy him. I think he wanted to go, you know. Then we both took him to the Station, Len muttering threats the whole time. Len didn't want to be seen with him, so he went to the office and clocked on for duty. I took him to the platform. Len knew there was one train with evacuees going to the Oxford area, and another going to the West. I looked at them both. One seemed to have a lot of teachers, some of them carrying cases. Not very promising. I chose the other—I don't know which it was. There were two teachers, but they were obviously just loading the kids on to the train. When they both got on to check the carriages, I whispered: "Remember, not a word who you are. Think up a nice new name! Find yourself a nice family to live with!" Then I shoved him forward, and made myself scarce. I watched him go up to the group, and get on the train. I waited till it drew out. It seemed an age. Then I went back home—to all the business of declaring Mary missing. By lunch-time Len had been to the hospital and identified the body. By evening there was just the three of us in the house, and I was congratulating myself. Really it all went wonderfully smoothly!'

Simon looked at her—fat, comfortable, amiable—'a good sort'. And he saw beneath the surface amiability, the comfortable self-approval, a moral vacuum more frightening than any of Len's casual brutalities or mean-spirited hatreds. Without sense of right or wrong, without love or sense of responsibility, there was in her mind only an abyss of complacency and self-love which made the blood run cold and numbed the heart. It was with this woman, rather than the Cutheridges, that he might have dragged out his childhood and youth. His heart sang out with gratitude at his deliverance. He said:

'You really managed it admirably.'

'Yes, didn't I? You could say it turned out well for all concerned. I bet Ted found some country family that looked after him all right. It's better for kids growing up in the country, isn't it? And I was shot of him. Mind you, I had a nasty moment a little later on.'

'What was that?'

'It was late that evening, and we were all in the house. The bereaved family. Len was wondering how he was going to tell Davey when he went to visit him. And while we were sitting there, talking low (as was only respectable, Ma thought), Ma asked about getting Ted away. She said "Good riddance to bad rubbish", in her pleasant way. She asked how I'd joined him on to a party, and I told her, and I said it really felt like a burden physically lifted off my shoulders as I saw him walk down that platform, his little case in his hand, his satchel on his back. And Ma thundered: "You didn't send him off with his satchel?" ' Connie Simmeter laughed and laughed. 'Do you know what I'd done?'

'You'd sent him off with a satchel with his name in it.'

'That's right! After all our precautions! I didn't know his bloody name was in it. It was Mary did all that kind of thing for him. Typical of her to write his name in it, in indelible ink, when he started school. We lived in fear for days. Len came over here, to Islington, to look for another house and a new job—not hard then, with everyone away at the war. But every night before we moved we expected a visit from the police, or at least a welfare officer. "Edward Mandel, c/o Simmeter," that's what she'd written in the satchel. You'd think with a name like Simmeter they'd have been able to trace us easily enough, wouldn't you? I don't know what it was—everything was chaos in those days, so perhaps there was just a mix-up and everyone thought someone else was investigating it. Or perhaps he realized the danger himself, and blacked it out, or said the satchel was another boy's. Anything could have happened.'

'Yes, anything could,' said Simon. 'In point of fact I threw the satchel out of the train window. Thank God—I threw it away. Good night, Miss Simmeter.'

Thinking over the interview later, as he often did, Simon was always glad he hadn't called her "Mother".

CHAPTER 18

During the early 'eighties, the London Zoo went through something of a crisis. Or, as several of the board preferred to put it, it was in a crisis situation (Simon was never quite sure whether this made it sound more or less critical). Admission fees had been drastically raised, and the number of visitors had correspondingly fallen. Finances were rocky, and many of the Zoo's traditional policies were called into question. Its affairs appeared all too often in *Private Eye*, and circulars were sent to all the staff which had an almost wartime sound to them, warning them against loose talk. A well-loved animal moped itself to death in captivity, and the Zoo's whole approach to the custody of wildlife became a matter of public debate. A shake-up was necessary—new investment policies, new houses for many categories of animals, a new relationship with the visitors. The governing board had to be shaken out of its complacency. One of the new members of the Board was Sir Isaiah Mandel.

He was by then semi-retired from the family businesses, and very rich indeed. Semi-retired, he would explain with a great laugh to anyone who asked, meant that he only interfered when he felt like it. The family business which had once been a chain of jewellery shops had expanded and diversified into so many fields of activity that no one (apart, perhaps, from Sir Isaiah himself) could have come up with a list of each and every pie that the firm had a finger in. Nor had business been the only field of Sir Isaiah's activities: he was on the board of the National Theatre, had been chairman of the Parole Board, and was often to be seen sleeping at Glyndebourne. He had been put on the board of the Zoo to shake things up.

He went about things fairly unobtrusively. In the weeks after his appointment he was to be seen walking around the

Zoo—a paunchy, energetic figure, with a bald head and a hearty manner, peering, surveying, and noting down. He talked to keepers and members of the public—even, it was rumoured, to some of the animals as well. He examined the power structure, stewed over the books, and generally seemed to be making a thorough job of whatever he was doing. In 1983 Simon was acting head of the scientific staff, and in November of that year Sir Isaiah invited him for lunch in a little restaurant in Mayfair.

Sir Isaiah was very genial, and the lunch was extremely good. Simon noted that Sir Isaiah seemed to acknowledge no dietary restrictions. He had done his homework on the most obvious aspects of Simon's private life, and questioned him pleasantly about it while they read the menu.

'Wife's an actress, isn't she?' 'Course she is. Seen her often. What was the name of that television show? *Three into Two*. That was it. Not bad. They made it sound funny even when it wasn't. Got any more series coming up, has she? . . . '

There were no flies on Sir Isaiah. As soon as they had ordered, he plunged straight into Zoo business—questioning, probing, suggesting, floating ideas and possibilities. 'Remember, I'm an outsider,' he said several times; 'I'm just trying to find out what can and what can't be done.' Simon applauded some of his ideas, expressed quiet scepticism about others, pointed to consequences and side-effects that Sir Isaiah had not taken into account. Sir Isaiah ate heartily, but did not let it interfere with his inquisition. He clearly did not go in for the type of business lunch where the only business aspect is that it is a business that pays the bill. Simon worked for his food. By the time they came to coffee and brandy Sir Isaiah was jotting down notes.

'I'm new to animals,' he said. 'Perhaps I make that all too obvious, do I? I'm a London boy. My parents didn't even encourage pets. Now I believe you're a countryman, aren't you?'

'Pretty much,' said Simon. 'I was born in London, but I was evacuated to Gloucestershire when I was about five. I stayed on and grew up there.'

'I see. Parents killed, eh?'

'No. I suppose you could say that they weren't really interested. As a matter of fact, I believe you once knew my mother. Her name is Connie Simmeter.'

Sir Isaiah wrinkled his forehead.

'Don't think so . . . Can't say I recall . . . Wait a minute! Good heavens! Connie! Practically my first love. Only my second or third, anyway. Bit of a disaster, as it turned out . . . Good Lord! You don't mean to say that you—'

'She only had the one child.'

'Well, heavens above! What a coincidence!' A slightly roguish smile suddenly wreathed his face. 'Things catch up with one, don't they? Quite like a Sunday newspaper story, isn't it? She was a sharp little thing, was Connie. Do you know, she screwed five pounds a week out of my parents for eighteen years? I never heard the last of that, I can tell you.' He banged his head, as a thought struck him. 'And you say she didn't bring you up most of the time?'

'Not after I was five. I'm afraid your parents were had.'

'They were, weren't they? Well and truly fleeced. It wasn't often *that* happened. It all turned out pretty well, though, didn't it? For you, I mean?'

Sir Isaiah looked at his watch, and decided not to wait for an answer.

'Good Lord, is that the time? I've got a meeting of the governors of the Nat in half an hour's time. Well, it's been an interesting talk. You've given me lots of info, and a lot to think over. I expect our paths will cross at meetings and suchlike.' He got up, and waiters hovered around him. He hesitated, seeming to think that something more was required. He decided to shake Simon by the hand. 'You must come to dinner some evening. Bring the wife. I'll get my secretary to ring and arrange a date.'

And he bustled out to a waiting taxi. Simon nodded to the manager, and walked briskly back to the Zoo. He had a busy afternoon ahead of him. A giraffe was arriving from a zoo in Southern France, to be mated with one at Regent's Park. Simon didn't anticipate any problems. These things arranged themselves with so much less fuss in the animal world.